Cover design by Bill Toth.

Book design by Iris Bass.

Author photograph by D. L. Drake.

David Handler

AVAILABLE
PRESS

BALLANTINE BOOKS • NEW YORK

For Mino

1972

Chapter One

Danny got off the truck at dusk. It was an organic vegetable truck headed for a health food store in Laurel Canyon, and it dropped him at Sunset and Beverly Glen, where he took one step, slipped on the freshly-watered parkway grass, and took a world-class header. His duffel bag rolled back into the street where a car immediately ran over it and scattered its contents—his shirts, his socks, his size 44 Jockey-brand briefs—across Sunset Boulevard. Two teenagers zipping past in a Firebird convertible applauded.

Yes, the big fella was back in town.

It took him about thirty minutes to chase down his things and re-stow them. Then he brushed himself off, pulled his duffel over his shoulder, waddled over to the Bel Air Gate, and stuck out his thumb. Nobody picked him up. A lot of cars passed him on their way up the canyon. New, shiny cars. Porsches. Maseratis. Excaliburs. But nobody stopped. He sighed and started hoofing it.

The first thing Danny noticed was the smog. He could already feel it in his chest and his eyes. The second thing he noticed was how many new houses had been built on lots that he'd never thought *were* lots. Just little slivers of dirt and brush beside the road. Now they were great big fancy homes with Grecian columns and fountains and basketball hoops.

Home.

He trudged, thumb out. His workshirt stuck to him, and his torn, patched jeans were giving off the unmistakable aroma of manure from the truck. A long, black Cadillac passed him by. So did a Jaguar. Its driver honked at him to get out of the way. Instead of a toot its horn blatted out the opening bar of "If I Were A Rich Man" from *Fiddler on the Roof.*

Home, indeed.

He made the climb in an hour. The floodlights were on in front. Abe was on his hands and knees in the wide driveway, scrubbing the white cement with a brush. A bucket and gallon jug of industrial cleanser were beside him on the pavement. Abe's glasses, which hung around his neck on a chain, banged against his chest with each vigorous stroke of the brush.

Scrub-thwack. Scrub-thwack. Scrub-thwack.

His hair was grayer, his sideburns longer. His green paisley sportcoat was draped over the squared rear fin of the new black Cadillac that sat in the three-car garage. Abe hadn't gone in the house yet. It was his dream house, the one he'd built when they finally made it. He wouldn't go inside it if he found grease spots in its driveway.

Panting, Danny watched him from the curb and realized his father was one of the people who hadn't picked him up on his way up the canyon. "Hi Pop," he said quietly.

"Ya believe it?!" barked Abe, red-faced, not looking up from his scrubbing. "I told the stupid sonuvabitch to park in the *street!*"

"Which stupid sonuvabitch?" asked Danny, a little surprised that Abe seemed to be taking no notice that his only son hadn't been around for the past four years.

"Aw, that goddamned pool man. Left his goddamned truck in the driveway and now I've got grease spots all over the goddamned place. *Schmuck!* Grab the hose, kiddo."

Danny put down his duffel bag and fetched the hose, which had a chrome, trigger-activated power nozzle. Abe cradled his chin with the palm of his hand, then slowly and painfully pushed his head and neck to an erect position. Abe's back was dissolving. It kept him permanently stooped. Once there had been talk of surgery. But Abe refused it. Groaning, he struggled to his feet and moved out of the way. Danny shot the suds down to the curb.

"There you go, Pop. Good as new."

Abe shook his head, dissatisfied. "I'm gonna fire that *schmuck*. Ya believe it? Fourth one in three months."

Danny coiled the hose back up. "Is a pool man absolutely necessary?"

"Who else is gonna do it? Show me the list of candidates. You're gone. Poof. No card. Nothing . . ."

Danny cleared his throat. "Yeah, I—"

"And I," Abe broke in, "sure as hell didn't come this far to hang over the edge of the pool with a goddamned net in my hand and take a chance of my back freezing up and falling in and drowning! You home for good or what?"

"Came back for a wedding."

"Yours?"

"Mouse Stern. Remember him?"

"Sharp kid, sure. Old man was a doctor."

"Dentist."

"Same thing."

"He's marrying Wendy Waldman."

"Your Wendy Waldman?"

"She's not mine anymore."

Abe retrieved the bucket and cleanser and brush. There was more strain in his face than Danny remembered.

"Everything okay, Pop?"

"What would be wrong?"

"You seem kind of tense."

"*Tsuris.*"

"Anything in particular?"

"My *tsuris.*"

Danny nodded. Some things didn't change.

Abe's '57 Plymouth with the tail fins, plaid uphol-
stery, and pushbutton transmission was in the garage next to the Cadillac. So was a smaller car, under
a bright blue tarp.

"Is that my MG?" Danny asked.

His sixteenth birthday present. British racing green.
Fully equipped—wire wheels, AM–FM radio, Chev-
ron card.

"Of course," Abe replied. "Think we'd sell it?"

"No, no. Does it still run?"

"Of course. Think we'd let it die?" Abe grabbed his
coat, softened a little. "C'mon inside, kiddo. We'll
surprise mom, like the old days. I'll call out I'm home.
You'll walk in the door instead of me. Okay?"

They went up the flagstone steps to the giant red-
wood double doors. Other than the doors, the front
of the house was all glass. A row of hibiscus and pyr-
acantha shielded the living room from the street.

Abe kept the remote control unit for the garage door
on a little stand in the entry hall. He pointed it at
the garage and pushed the button. The door jumped
and lowered slowly. Abe watched it go down, a con-
tented smile on his face.

Coco heard them from the kitchen and came skit-
tering across the polished slate floor to greet them.
She was a dinky toy poodle, dark brown and very ex-
citable. She didn't recognize Danny and began to yap
at him. He picked her up, hoping to get her to stop.
He hadn't wanted them to get a poodle. He'd voted
for a big, solid retriever you could name Butch or Rex
and wrassle with. Ev, however, feared that such a

dog might hear the call of the wild one night and devour a member of the Levine family. Coco quieted down but began to squirm in his arms, her breathing rapid and shallow, her eyes glassy. She wanted to be put down. He obliged.

"Ev!" Abe called out. "I'm home!"

"I'm in the kitchen!" she called back.

Abe winked at Danny, gave him a shove.

The kitchen, breakfast area, and den were all sort of one big room separated by waist-high counters and facing the pool. There were sliding glass doors in the den and breakfast area.

Cronkite was giving the Vietnam fatality scoreboard update. America: 9, North Vietnam: 26,875. Another victorious week. At this rate they would kill over eleven million North Vietnamese by the year 1980. The war would still be going strong then. Nixon would still be president. Danny would be over thirty.

Ev wore an apron over her dress and plush blue slippers Danny gave her for Chanuka when he was in junior high. Her hands were buried in a large Pyrex bowl filled with raw hamburger meat, egg, and oatmeal. Meat loaf. Danny's stomach growled. He hadn't eaten for a whole day, except for those four Baby Ruths in Kettleman City.

"Take a piece of cheese, Abe," she said, not looking up. "I'm running late."

Danny cut himself a generous slab of Longhorn cheddar and flopped down in one of the club chairs clumped around the breakfast table. He forgot that the casters rolled on the slate floor and had to brake himself with his heels or he would have rolled right out the sliding glass door into the pool and sunk to the bottom and drowned.

"Did you talk to Irv about his proposal?" Ev asked, still not looking up.

Danny bit into his cheese. "Which proposal is that, Mom?"

Ev froze. Her eyes widened. She looked up, saw him there. Then she clutched at her chest and fainted. She landed with a thud.

"You been taking your estrogen, Ev?" Abe asked her after he and Danny carried her upstairs and waved ammonia under her nose.

"Yes," she said.

"What about your iron?"

She had more lines in her face. Her red curls had gray in them now. How odd that the two of them had aged so much, reflected Danny. *He* was the one who'd been out there experiencing and growing.

Abe's heating pad was waiting for him on his side of the bed. A copy of the collected essays of Henry David Thoreau was on his nightstand. Ev was still reading *The Source* by James Michener.

"Goddamned hysterectomy," said Abe. "That's what it is. Never used to have problems."

"That's got nothing to do with it. I've told you a million times not to play your tricks on me."

"Just teasing ya. Can't I tease ya anymore?"

"You never *could*. Twenty-five years I've been telling you."

She held her arms out to Danny. He leaned down and hugged her. She hugged him back.

"Are you home for good, sweetheart?"

"Actually, I—"

"Mouse Stern is getting married," Abe answered. "And guess who? Wendy Waldman."

"His Wendy Waldman?"

"She's not his anymore."

The three of them sat in silence on the bed, not quite ready to move on to some of the tougher questions, like, say, where the hell he'd been, and was he finally ready to take his spot.

Abe sniffed at him and made a face. "When's the

last time you had a bath? Smell like you were on the back of a hay wagon."

"Actually, it was a—"

"Go grab yourself one. And do something about that beard, will ya? Scared your mom half to death."

Nothing in Danny's room had been disturbed. The calendar page on his desk was still turned to June 1968. His Harding High and Dodger pennants and humorous "No Parking" and "Men's Room" signs were still affixed to the cork-paneled wall, along with the "Pat Paulsen for President" sticker and the framed team picture of the rough, tough, 1966 Harding Blue Warriors varsity football squad. Danny, the team captain, stood in the front row in full pads and game uniform, squinting at the camera, his hair a whorl of erect, inch-high bristles. He looked like a wild boar. He'd been known as Fireplug Levine then, or simply Plug. Nobody called him Plug anymore. Next to him stood Rick Farber, his quarterback and student body president. Rachel Stern's steady boyfriend—and fiancé, last he'd heard. Big Rick's smile was confident and sure. His blond hair tumbled into a loose comma over his forehead. It was all so uncomplicated for Big Rick. *"Am I wrong?"* That's what he always said—when he wasn't wrong, and he knew it, and you darned well better know it, too. Big Rick. What an asshole.

Danny's weights and pressing bench were just where he'd left them. So was his old violin. Music stand. Lava lamp. Bongos. Record player. Ancient high school record collection: Tijuana Brass, New Christy Minstrels, Limelighters, the theme from *The Magnificent Seven*. This was the place. Right here. This was where he had dreamed that with Rachel Stern by his side he would one day become the very first Jewish president of the United States. Just had to believe Coach K's Third Winning Principle: *I am capable of achieving far more than I have the faintest conception of trying to do.* And

bear in mind Coach K's Fourth Winning Principle:
Check both feet daily for topical fungi. Your opponent does.

Danny stripped, padded into his bathroom, and
looked at himself in the mirror. His body, which once
had heaved with several tons of excess blubber, had
now settled into a state where, well, he thought it
was not out of line to think of himself as ample. That
was a nice word for it.

His hair wasn't particularly long. The black curls got
too tangled and knotted on the road for him to let
them go. But his beard was bushy and grew halfway
down his neck. He found scissors in a drawer and
trimmed it so that it was even with his jawline. Then
he found his old Remington electric shaver—the one
that could trim and shape and even re-charge itself without being told to—flicked it on and pressed it against
his neck. There was a whole lot of noise, but not much
else. He pressed down harder—Varooooom—and
shaved a nice, wide stripe up through his beard to his
cheekbone. Danny stared at himself in the mirror and
sighed. He looked like Tony the Tiger.

Oh well, he *had* sort of wondered what was
underneath.

He showered, lathered up, and shaved once, twice,
three times with a real razor until his face was bare
and pink and slick.

He looked exactly the same as when he left. The road
hadn't left a mark. *No difference.*

Unhappily Danny dumped his duffel on the bedroom floor in search of something that didn't have
tire marks on it.

"Kitchen to kiddo. Dinner, kiddo. Dinner."

Danny flicked the talk button on the intercom above
his desk. "Kiddo to kitchen," he responded. "Ten-four."

He put on a fresh T-shirt and jeans. Toilet paper
stopped the blood oozing from his chin and upper
lip. He padded downstairs barefoot, cleaner than he'd
been since he left Sweden. The house was clean, too.

Not a speck of dirt on the floor to stick to his feet. A little different from that peach picker's shack he'd been living in for the past three months. He and two other guys, both of them named Jorge. There was cold beer in the refrigerator. He opened one.

They were eating at the outside table, the lights of the city twinkling below. They stopped talking when he came out. Coco yapped at him again. Ev shushed her.

His old Flintstones mug sat at his place at the table. Fred. Barney. Wilma. Dino. He stared at it.

"Found it in the attic last summer," Abe said, grinning. "Thought you'd get a kick out of it."

"I don't remember us having an attic."

Danny picked it up, started to empty his beer into it, stopped himself, went inside and came back out with a grown-up glass. This he poured his beer into. Then he sat.

"Ah, there's our boy, Ev," exclaimed Abe, beaming. "Good. Let's eat."

Chapter Two

"Gimme Some Lovin' " by the Spencer Davis Group
was pounding away on the tinny sound system. The
dancer, a big-boned blonde equipped with immense,
siliconed breasts, was grinding her hips directly over
them. She had daisies and peace signs painted all over
her body. They glowed in the black lights that were
blinking on and off to the beat. Blinking. Blinking.
Half-blinding Danny. Even so, there was no mistak-
ing what he saw now:

Mouse Stern, cackling, face gleaming with sweat, was
slipping a ten-dollar bill into her g-string.

For this Mouse got a private show. First she wiggled her tongue at him. Then she fell to her knees
and shook her breasts at him, over him, around him,
enveloping the little guy's entire head for a second.

"Shake 'em, big mama!" he cried, his voice muffled
by the mammaries. "Shake 'em!"

And then the show was over, and she was prancing
off the little stage, and getting a big, big hand from
everybody, especially Mouse's stag party, made up of
the groom-to-be and his best man, Danny Levine.

Mouse whooped, snapped his fingers for another

round of whiskeys and beers, and puffed on his foot-long cigar. "This, boychick," he proclaimed expansively, "is living."

Yes, it was Mouse's night. So far they'd been to Farmer's Market, where they read comic books and girlie magazines and bought several fine specimens of plastic vomit. Then on to Pinks, where they each wolfed down three franks topped with chili, raw onion, and jalapeño peppers. Then to a Rexall, where Mouse got himself a large bottle of Maalox. And now here, the Pink Pussycat, on the Sunset Strip. Danny had never seen Mouse so happy. He'd also never seen him part with a ten-dollar bill so freely.

Mouse hunched excitedly in his chair, his bony shoulders up to his ears. He wore all black—a black cardigan over a black shirt, black slacks, and glossy black ankle boots. He'd started combing his dark brown hair forward to cover the premature balding at his temples. Actually, Mouse wasn't a bad-looking guy. He'd finally grown into his nose and ears. Well, maybe his ears a little more than his nose. And when he stood up good and straight he was a legit five feet two.

"Man oh man," he gushed. "I like them big mammas. Got a boner out to Oxnard just thinking about it. You'd have to peel me off the ceiling, but what a way to go, huh, boychick?"

"Stern, you never change," Danny said. "Pound for pound, you're still the classiest guy I've ever met."

Their drinks came. Mouse raised his shot glass. Danny did the same.

"Here's to tits," said Mouse.

"Here's to Wendy," corrected Danny.

"Here's to Wendy's tits."

They gulped down the whiskey and washed it down with house draft.

Danny sat back, puffed on his own foot-long cigar. "I don't mean to be an asshole, but I distinctly recall us agreeing on the beach at Malibu in the summer of

'62 that someday we'd like to stick a firecracker up
Wendy Waldman's . . . up her . . ."

"*Cunt*, Levine," Mouse said, biting the word off.

". . . And light it."

"Still intend to. Only now it's gonna be legal." He
cackled. "Tell me the truth, Levine. I always figured
. . . I mean, you ever bang her? All those years you
went out together?"

Danny hesitated, cleared his throat. "No, Stern.
Never did. Closest I ever got was second base, one
night when we were on her bed and Rabbi and
Mrs. Waldman were in the living room watching
Bonanza."

Mouse downed his beer, pleased. "I know. That's
what she told me. Good to see you again, Levine.
Missed you. You're still the only person in the world
I completely trust. See, anybody who has a clam, anybody who I do business with, it's always ulterior motives, it's conditions, it's price tags. You and me, we
don't have that between us. See any of the old gang
since you been back?"

"What old gang is that?"

"The Wasp. Biddle."

"Newt? No. I sort of needed to get away from him.
That happens, from time to time."

It certainly did. There was that first time, when
Danny and Newt got caught stealing the tape recorder. There was a second time, when Newt called
Danny a fascist for going out for football. And then
there was now.

"Last time I saw him he was working the swap
meets," Danny said, "selling off the old Long Island
family treasures. His dad's driving a cab, living in Silver Lake. His mom finally drank herself to death."

Danny could not forget the night Mrs. Biddle died.
He and Newt were listening to *Disraeli Gears* by
Cream in the dingy living room of the Biddles' house
on Kelton when the phone rang.

Newt had just stared at it. "I suppose that's it," he said. "Father calling from the hospital to say she's slipping fast, that I'd better come right away."

The phone kept ringing.

"Aren't you gonna answer it?" Danny finally asked.

Newt shook his head. "She's been dead for a long time. There's no point in pretending otherwise. It would be dishonest. I refuse to be dishonest."

That was Newt for you.

Mouse drained his beer. "Didn't you live with him in that dump on Kelton for a while?"

"We were in business together, briefly. Lids. Tabs. Just enough to break even. And scramble our brains pretty thoroughly."

And yet, Danny reflected, he and Newt had come to grips with a lot of major truths. There was, for instance, the night on orange sunshine when they'd finally, once and for all, discovered the meaning of life: Beefaroni.

"Never had any use for acid," Mouse sniffed. "Or Biddle. Whole family's on a stairway going nowhere."

"That's one way of looking at it. In his own way, Newt's a visionary."

"Like I said—a loser. Not like us. Gonna go to work for the old man?"

Eight Japanese businessmen came into the club and sat at two tables next to them, jabbering.

Danny shrugged. "Dunno."

"Don't shit me. He built it for you. How many Pier West outlets has he got now?"

"Twenty-seven, I think."

"Jesus. To think he started with one lousy stationery store. Pay attention when he talks to you, boychick. Business, he knows." Mouse snapped his fingers for another round, leaned forward on the wobbly table. "You're a Jew, Levine. A striver. A battler. A survivor. You've got to keep that battle going. It's your nature. And I'll tell you something: *You can't change your nature.*"

"I know," Danny said. "I tried. Hard."

"What's your status, Vietnam-wise?"

"Lawyer got me off. Migraines."

"Same here. Allergies. Good thing, too. I hear the draft board's starting to get around to the white guys." Mouse gulped his fresh drink. "Face it, Levine. You fucked around for a while. Experimented. Traveled. Now it's time to start battling, like I am."

"What exactly are you doing?"

"I'm Annie Mott's fair-haired boy," he said proudly.

"Who's Annie Mott?"

"You never heard of her?" he demanded, flabbergasted. "What planet you been on? She's *the* hottest talent agent in the business. Half the young guys in town would pay *her* to be her assistant, just for the chance to learn the ropes from her. Believe me, it wasn't easy getting this job. I'm working in the agency mailroom, see. Waiting for any chance. Word gets out Annie Mott's looking for a new boy. Last one moved right into a production v.p. job at Universal. Twenty-six years old. Now, this is no easy woman to work for. She's an ugly, fat, disgusting dyke, frankly. And *nasty*. She tries out every young guy in the place. One a day. Ten, twelve of 'em. Rejects 'em all. Comes my turn, I show up bright and early, I say 'Can I get your coffee for you this morning, Miss Mott?' And she says, 'I'm Annie Mott! I don't take coffee! I take hot milk!' Fine, so I bring her a cup of hot milk. And she says 'I'm Annie Mott! I don't take a whole cup of hot milk! I take a half-cup!' 'What do I do with the other half?' I says. She says, 'Figure it out. If you don't have initiative, I don't want you.' So, I calmly poured half of it all over her head. She hired me on the spot. Confirmed something I've suspected for a long, long time—the movie business and I were made for each other." Mouse puffed on his cigar. "This wedding, it's gonna be very important for me."

"It's a big step," Danny agreed.

"That old man of Wendy's is hooked into every rich Jew in West L.A. If I can raise just five thou from each of 'em, I'll have enough to bankroll my first feature. I'm gonna independent produce 'em, see. That's my plan. Then there'll be no stopping me. Then I'll be tasting the real pussy. Jane Fonda . . . Candy Bergen . . ."

"What about Wendy?"

"What about her?"

"You're getting married to her tomorrow."

"So?"

"Aren't you . . . don't you *love* her?"

"Wake up, will ya Levine? It's 1972. You *won't* get blood poisoning from wearing dark socks to gym class. Babe Ruth *didn't* miss half of the 1925 season because he got sick from eating too many hot dogs. People *don't* fall in love. They use each other. I'm only twenty-three years old. The older people, they want to see I'm serious and responsible before they invest in me. They want to see I'm *married*."

"Does Wendy know how you feel?" asked Danny, incredulous.

"Wendy wants a husband. One with a future. And I've made a remarkable discovery about women, Levine. Deep down inside, all they really, truly care about is clothes and money and not having to get out of bed too early."

"It's nice to see the women's movement is rubbing off on you, Stern."

"What, you don't agree?"

"Look, I'm not judging you. I just . . ."

"Go ahead. Say it."

"Well, my idea of a serious relationship is somebody who has a mind of her own. You know, ideas, tastes, interests. Somebody stimulating."

"Uh-huh. Meet anyone like that lately?"

"No, not lately," he confessed.

"My point exactly."

"But I haven't been looking," Danny pointed out. "I'm sort of off women."

Mouse's eyes widened. "You're not . . . ?"

"Oh no, no, no. Just traveling light, I guess you could say."

That was one way of looking at it. Another was that Danny was the only guy in recorded history with four limbs and no visible running sores who had spent an entire year in Europe without once getting laid. He just wasn't the kind of guy girls wanted to have a wild sexual adventure with. He was more the kind they approached for directions to the train station.

Mouse got to his feet. "C'mon, Levine. Let's blow this dump."

"Just as soon as I unstick my feet from the floor," agreed Danny.

There were prostitutes and winos out on the sidewalk. The Strip was home now to head shops and dirty bookstores and sleazy clubs like the one they'd just been in.

"Getting pretty seedy around here," Danny observed.

"Strip was always seedy," Mouse said. "Your folks just never brought you here."

"That's not true. See where that record store is? Used to be a Will Wright's. Had the best hot fudge sundae around."

"No way. C.C. Brown's on Hollywood Boulevard."

"Will Wright's chopped their own nuts right on the spot."

"C.C. Brown's had the best hot fudge. Still does."

"And I saw Michael Rennie, the actor, there once. He was eating a—"

"Levine?"

"Yeah, Stern?"

"We're too young for nostalgia."

Danny's MG was parked at the curb, top down. They hopped in and Danny started her up.

"Hey, where's your cap?" demanded Mouse.

In the old days Danny had worn a pigskin racing cap when he was behind the wheel. It had been his trademark.

"It's in the glove compartment," he said. "Where it belongs."

"Nonsense." Mouse opened the glove compartment and pulled it out. "Put it on at once."

"I don't want to wear it, Stern."

"I insist. It's my party. C'mon."

Danny sighed, put the cap on. It fit snugly, what with his hair being curlier now. "Feel like a real Jewish prince," he muttered.

"You *are* a real Jewish prince. Roll around in it. Like with this car. This is nice."

"Newt always said it was a car for people who don't know anything about cars."

"Is it?"

"I don't know. I don't know anything about cars."

Danny took Laurel Canyon up to Lookout Mountain, the radio blaring. It felt good to be behind the wheel again. He loved the way the MG hugged the curves. Loved its throaty roar, the wind, the speed.

When they got to the top of the mountain, he pulled off to the shoulder. They sat there, gazing down at the lights and the even rows of boulevards.

"Someday, boychick," Mouse intoned like an old Jew, "this will all be yours." Then he cackled, opened his door, and tumbled out. "Gotta take a piss."

"Swordfight?"

"You're on."

"So listen, Levine," said Mouse, as they thrusted and parried urine streams in the bushes. "Far be it from me to pimp for somebody, but if you're really interested in somebody spiky and headstrong and stubborn, there's always Baby Snooks."

"Your sister Rachel?"

"I happen to know she's available." He glanced up at Danny. "And I happen to know you had a thing for her."

One of the great mysteries of modern science, Danny felt, was how the same two humans, Dr. and Mrs. Stern, had produced both Mouse and Rachel. Rachel was nothing like her brother. She was tall, blond, blue-eyed, athletic, pretty, sweet, popular. Her nose was small, her teeth straight, her cheeks dimpled. Rachel was the Homecoming Queen. The Head Cheerleader. The Miss Everything. She was even smart. Danny had loved her desperately. Worshipped her year after year after year from a very short, very painful distance. She'd always been Rick Farber's girl. Danny had been the guy who went out with her best friend, Wendy Waldman. At first, he thought about Rachel a lot when he was on the road. But as he saw and experienced more of the real world out there, he finally outgrew her. Rachel was behind him now. She was *then*. She was laughter and sunshine and no cares. She was Malibu Rachel—bikini, towel, and powder blue Mustang convertible sold separately.

Twice during the evening he'd asked Mouse how she was doing—strictly out of curiosity—but both times the little guy's face had darkened and he'd changed the subject.

"I win!" Mouse cried triumphantly as Danny's stream flickered and died out.

They zipped up and staggered back to the car.

"So, don't tell me Rachel finally broke up with Big Rick after all these years."

"Permanently. He's dead."

"What?!"

"Hanged himself last winter in the SC law library. Climbed right up on a pile of torts and did himself in."

"B-but why?"

"He left a note. Just three words. 'Am I wrong?' "
Danny shuddered. "Wow," he said hoarsely.

"Know what he wrote in my senior yearbook?
'Roses are red, violets are blue. Your ears are big, and
so is your nose.' I never forgot it. That's the Rick
Farber I knew. I don't know what she saw in him."

"How is she . . . how did she handle it?"

"Not so good. Lives by herself in a shack in Venice. Doesn't see anybody. She worries me. Good opportunity for you though."

"Sometimes, Stern, I'm reminded why this is only
a two-man stag party."

They sat and stared at the lights below.

"Am I wrong?"

"Levine?" Mouse said softly.

"Yeah, Stern?"

"What if *we're* wrong?"

"About what?"

"What if there's something else out there?"

"There isn't," Danny said quietly. "I checked."

Chapter Three

Mouse Stern and Wendy Waldman were married in the back yard of the dignified, two-story red brick home on Charing Cross that the Beverly Glen congregation gave to Rabbi Waldman. It was a half-mile away from the temple, and it was where Danny and Wendy first had sex together.

Being the best man, Danny got there early. Rabbi Waldman greeted him at the front door. The rabbi was deeply tanned and had wavy black hair. He wore a trim, European-style gray suit with a burgundy-and-white-striped tie. He seemed elated.

"Well, well, young fellow," he exclaimed as he pumped Danny's hand. "The last time I saw you you were in a letterman's sweater."

"This certainly is a happy day," observed Danny.

"It is indeed. It makes me very happy to see two young people embracing the institution of marriage. It seems like all you kids want to do is tear things down."

"It's nothing personal, sir," Danny said, as he looked around for someone his own age.

"PLUG-WUG!" he heard Wendy cry. "IT'S MY PLUG-WUG!"

Danny winced. He'd never liked her pet name for him—it sounded like a sink unstopping.

She was at the top of the stairs. She started down. He started up. They met halfway and she gave him a big hug-wug. She wore a long white gown and had flowers in her hair, which she no longer wore in a flip. She no longer wore white lip gloss or heavy black eyeliner either. She'd lost a few pounds in the hips and caboose. Her eyes were wide, her lips full. She looked nice.

"Plug-wug," she whispered in his ear.

"Little Gal," he whispered back.

"Know what I was trying to figure out last night?"

"Who, if anyone, is going to vote for George Mc-Govern in November?"

"No, silly. Why we broke up."

Because she kept wanting to make plans. Plans for next month, for next year, for the year 2023. Because she wasn't Rachel.

"Beats me," Danny replied, smiling. "I'm real happy for you, Little Gal."

"You are?" She seemed surprised. "Why thank you, Wuggy. That's very *mature* of you."

"It is?"

She rushed off to greet some old aunt.

Mouse seemed amazingly calm. He led Danny upstairs to Wendy's bedroom, where their outfits were hanging from the closet door in plastic. She'd ditched the John, Paul, George, and Ringo dolls. Otherwise, her room looked the same.

The movie *Casablanca* was very popular that summer. Mouse had chosen for them to wear old-fashioned white dinner jackets and black tuxedo pants so they'd look just like Bogart had in the movie. Personally Danny thought the two of them together looked more like Peter Lorre and Sydney Greenstreet. They clipped on their bow ties in Wendy's bathroom, standing shoulder to shoulder in front of the mirror.

Danny's eyes avoided the toilet before which he and Wendy had stood, naked, and ceremonially flushed their very first used Trojan. She had worn a plaid wool skirt to school that day. And a pink mohair sweater. And penny loafers and knee socks with stockings under them.

"Looking forward to hitting the beach in Acapulco?" Danny asked.

"I don't like being away from the agency action, but I guess you gotta go. I mean they expect it, right?" He sniffed at Danny. "What's that you got on?"

"Uh . . . English Leather. Found an old bottle in my medicine chest. No good?"

"No, no. It's fine—as long as you don't mind smelling like a guy who's been dead for three days in the trunk of a Chevy Nova." He handed Danny a small jewelry box. "Here's the ring. And this one is for you, Levine." It was another jewelry box, a longer one. "Traditional for the best man to get a gift," Mouse explained.

It was a wristwatch, not quite as large as a lunchbox. Instead of a dial with hands it gave the time digitally, the numbers blinking on and off when you pressed the right button.

"Here, it's got an alarm, too."

"Gee, thanks, Stern." Danny punched him on the shoulder. "Nervous?"

"Uh-uh. Should I be?"

They started downstairs. The maid of honor was down there now, talking to Rabbi Waldman. Danny froze when he caught sight of Rachel across the room. She was so *thin*. Gaunt almost. She wore a plain, shapeless white dress. Her beautiful shiny blond hair was twisted into tight braids. Her legs were bare and unshaven. Danny flashed on sitting next to her every day in student government, when she'd been head cheerleader and he boys' league president. How he'd loved to gaze at her—the way she nibbled on her pen,

brow furrowed, when she was concentrating. The way
she assertively raised her chin just before she asked
to be recognized by the chairman, Big Rick. The way
she gracefully crossed and uncrossed her silken legs
when she got up and down, smoothed her skirt, swept
back those few loose hairs from her pony tail. Gazing at her perfectly turned wrists, fingers, ankles.
Gazing . . .

She wasn't that Rachel anymore.

"I'll admit she needs a little fattening up," said
Mouse. "And a Lady Schick wouldn't hurt, either.
But she still has a lovely complexion. Never a single
blackhead."

She hugged him tightly and he hugged her back,
though she was so thin and delicate he thought he
might crush her if he hugged her too hard. He released her and held her at arm's length. There was
an air of melancholy about her. Her blue eyes were
sunk deep in their sockets and had dark circles around
them. Big Rick's death had definitely done a number
on her.

"Danny Levine has curly hair," she said, her voice
huskier than he remembered it.

"I . . . I . . ." The words caught in Danny's throat.
His heart was pounding. He was weak in the knees.
He couldn't believe it. "I stopped using Brylcreem,"
he finally got out, his voice soaring three octaves.

"Say, Levine," kidded Mouse. "I didn't know your
voice was still changing."

Danny flushed beet red. Rachel laughed, and for a
second the sunlight in her eyes broke through.

"Hey, call the *Times*," exclaimed Mouse. "Baby
Snooks is *laughing*. All she usually does is mope and
starve and call me a sexist pig. You're good for her,
Levine."

The sliding glass door to the patio had been opened.
There was laughter and music coming from out there
now.

With it came a cloud. It passed over Rachel's eyes.
Her face was gloomy again.

Mouse straightened his bow tie and grimaced.
"C'mon," he said toughly. "Let's get this dirty business out of the way."

A cage with two white lovebirds in it was floating
in the deep end of the swimming pool. The *chupa*
had been erected on the lawn. A musician was playing
"Proud Mary" by Creedence Clearwater Revival on
a small electric organ that also produced the sounds of
a bass guitar, drums, and cowbell. There was a bar,
but it wasn't open yet. Dr. Stern was handling the liquor, and liquor cost money.

There were about a hundred guests. Other than
Danny, Rachel, and the happy couple, none were under fifty. But something had happened to old Jews
while Danny had been away. No more little yellow
men in baggy blue suits, with foreign accents and hair
growing out of their ears. No more round old women
in black dresses and orthopedic shoes. These old men
wore muttonchop sideburns, tight flared trousers and
flowered ties wide as lobster bibs. They even carried
little leather purses. The women wore short skirts and
go-go boots and love beads. Their skin was tanned,
their hair flowed free. Many of the oldsters were out
on the portable dance floor, grinding their pelvises to
Creedence, getting down.

It was, Danny thought, disgusting.

How could his voice have cracked like that?

He began to mill around, remembering how much
he hated these big affairs. When he was younger he
hated them because nobody talked to him and he felt
like a fat oaf and always managed to do something totally spazy. Now that he'd grown up, seen things,
acquired his own values and attitudes, he realized he
hated them because nobody talked to him and he felt
like a fat oaf and always managed to do something totally spazy.

He kept as far away from the pool as he could, certain that if he got within six feet of it, he'd fall in.

At a signal from Rabbi Waldman, the organist switched to somber, *shul* music. The dancers took their seats. Danny and Mouse took their places, as did Rachel. And the show began.

Mouse and Wendy had written their own vows.

Hers: "My life as a woman grows. Trembling, I step forward into the sunlight. As one, but now two. Heart full. Senses alive. Hold me. Touch me. See me. Feel me. Marry me. I love you, Michael."

His: "Wendy, I promise to make you happy until we both grow old and die."

Danny handed him the ring. The rabbi spoke. Mouse stepped on the glass and it broke and they were married. It was over very fast. A cameraman recorded it on videotape, which was the new thing.

Then champagne was poured. A plastic wine goblet was pressed into Danny's hand and he found himself being pushed up onto the little stage to the microphone. The best man, he was told, delivered the toast. The guests sat attentively at the white covered tables, glasses held high, waiting for him to speak.

Danny looked out at them and cleared his throat. "I've known Mou . . . Mike and Wendy here for a long time. And I'd like you to join me in drinking to . . . to two people who are *terribly* right for each other. Well, that didn't come out right, but . . . *mazel tov.*"

"*Mazel tov,*" everyone chimed in.

And he drank. And missed his mouth by a good two inches. And poured his champagne down the front of his shirt and onto the floor. Everyone laughed. Danny laughed along sheepishly, turned, slipped on the puddle of champagne, and belly flopped onto the portable organ, which collapsed under his weight, wheezing out something that sounded like "My Dog Has Fleas."

The laughter rang in his ears. Mouse helped him up, cackling.

"Not to worry, Levine. Everything's rented. We knew you were coming."

Danny sought the refuge of his seat at the table nearest the stage and dabbed at his shirt with his napkin. When he looked up he discovered Rachel standing before him. She was watching the other guests, a sad, distant look on her face. The sunlight caught that bit of soft blond down above her upper lip.

He cleared his throat. "Weird scene, huh?"

"I haven't been around people for a while."

"Me either."

She looked at him now. "I hate weddings, actually."

"Me, too."

"They're so . . ."

"Fake?" he suggested.

"Real."

"Have a seat," he suggested. "If you like."

She sat.

"Well, they make a nice couple," he ventured.

"A nice couple of what?"

Danny didn't answer. Mouse wasn't kidding. She *had* gotten spiky.

"They don't actually like each other, per se," she said.

"Go on. They got married, didn't they?"

"So what?"

"Look, I know your big brother likes to talk real tough, but deep down—"

"Believe me. They don't like each other," she said sharply.

"Okay, fine." A wave of something washed over Danny. Suddenly he didn't want to talk to Rachel Stern. He didn't want to be back here. He shouldn't have come home at all. He should have gone north.

"Where have you been?" she said.

"Different places," he replied. "Europe. Ghana. Taught English there for a while."

"How was that?"

"Interesting. Challenging. Buggy. Worked on a tuna boat off Vancouver. That was cold. Went to school in San Francisco, briefly. About all I learned was I don't have much in common with mimes. For a while I was political, but—"

"Now you're apathetic just like everyone else."

"No, I just found it hard to stay so *concerned* for long. Too intense. Sort of like tripping, that way."

"You drop acid?"

"Not anymore. I flipped out."

"What was that like?"

Danny shifted uneasily. "You don't want to hear about it."

She shrugged. "Okay."

"Well . . . it started as a kind of chain reaction of mental images. Things popping into my head that I had no control over. First I started hearing the song 'Purple Haze' by Jimi Hendrix. Over and over. And then sirens. And then there was this old Jewish lady who said she lived somewhere off Fairfax, in a pink Spanish house. I got in the car and I tried to find her house. And I *did*. It turned out she lived with, well, out back I talked to . . ."

"You talked to who?"

Danny sighed. Other people had such fascinating, *deep* bummers. "Mister Ed," he confessed. "And it wasn't pleasant."

"Mister Ed, the horse?"

"Of course."

"Why 'of course'?"

"Don't you remember the theme song?"

"Sing it for me."

"Right here? No way. I want to hold onto what little dignity I still have."

Her sunken eyes searched his face. "You've changed, Danny."

"Me? How?"

Before she could answer him, Mouse and Wendy broke in on them, holding hands, giddy with relief and with their new-found wealth.

"You two have to dance," said Wendy.

"No way," Danny said. "I'm a terrible dancer. I hate it."

"So do I," agreed Rachel.

"You have to," insisted Mouse. "It's a tradition for the best man and maid of honor to dance. A nice frug, maybe? A mashed potato?"

"We're talking," Rachel said coldly.

"So I'll ask for a slow one," offered Mouse. "You can keep talking. Just sway, okay?"

Mouse asked the organist to play "As Time Goes By." Everyone cleared off the dance floor except Danny and Rachel. Danny took her hand, placed his other arm around her. Stiffly they began to dance.

"Thanks," he said.

"For what?" she said.

"For trying to get me out of this."

She frowned, puzzled. "What do you mean get *you* out of it?"

"You told your brother you hate dancing."

"I do hate it."

"C'mon, you won eight Dwighties when we were at Ike, and three—"

"Doesn't mean I liked it." She crinkled her nose. "Danny, are you actually wearing English Leather?"

"I-I might be," he said, reddening. Have to throw that damned bottle out. "How have I changed?"

"You seem . . . afraid."

"I am, actually. In fact, I'm facing my greatest fear in life."

"That's funny," she said. "So am I."

"Really? What's yours?"

Rachel looked away. "I don't know you well enough anymore to talk about it. Sorry."

"That's okay."

"How about yours?" she asked.

"Hey, no way," he said. "Fair is fair. You know, you've changed, too, Rachel. You're not the prettiest girl here anymore. You're the prettiest *woman.*"

She stiffened and shot him an icy, sidelong glance.

"That's not some kind of line," he explained hurriedly. "I just mean that we're not kids anymore. Either one of us. A lot has happened."

She nodded. And relaxed. And leaned into him a teeny bit. He liked the way she fit against him. And smelled. He'd always liked the way she smelled. Jean Naté. *Her* smell.

The guests were clustered around the dance floor watching them. It had been a while since Danny had seen the look he saw now on many of their faces: approval.

He felt hot and sweaty all of a sudden.

"What have *you* been doing?" he asked her.

"Not much. I fast. Do yoga. Read a lot."

"Are you blaming yourself for Rick's death?"

"Ayn Rand, mostly."

"Are you?" he pressed.

"You can't blame yourself for something someone else chooses to do. I understand that. Intellectually I do, at least. I just seem to have a lot of trouble being polite. I guess I don't much like people anymore. And I'm . . . I'm kind of mixed up about men."

"You mean . . . ?"

"Oh, no, no, no. It's just that I've only gone out with one guy my entire life and he killed himself. It's tough to get started again. Dating, for instance, is repulsive."

"I haven't done it myself in ages," Danny admitted. "I don't seem to have what women want from a guy."

"And what's that?"

"I used to think it was sex appeal. I guess it still is, partly. But what I think it really is, deep down, is answers."

"Answers?"

"Haven't got 'em."

"Well, don't date. You'll hate it. Some ass buys you dinner and the next thing you know he tries to stick his tongue down your throat."

"It might be a slightly different experience for me."

"Believe me, it's awful. I stopped."

"You working?"

"I counsel at the abortion clinic on Santa Monica and Barrington. And I'm in grad school at UCLA. I throw pots."

"I never knew you were an artist."

"Maybe I'm not."

"Don't kid me. You're Rachel Stern."

"So?"

"Whatever you do, you do it great."

She pulled back, startled. "Jesus," she said, shaking her head. "It's been a long time since I've heard *that.*"

Chapter Four

"Let's go, kiddo! Out of the sack! If the associate chief of personnel doesn't get out of bed on time, he can't expect his personnel to, can he?!"

Danny opened one eye. It was still dark in his room. His limbs were heavy with sleep, his throat thick.

Abe clapped his hands as punctuation. "We gotta be out the door by six if we wanna beat the traffic!" Clap. "La Mirada's murder!" Clap.

"Pop . . ."

"Yo, kiddo?"

"You always wake up this alert?"

"Always," Ev replied from the doorway. "He opens his eyes and he's awake."

"Maybe this isn't such a good idea," Danny groaned.

"Pull out now," Abe warned, "and your mom will be very disappointed."

Danny covered his head with the sheet and snuggled down.

"Ever tell ya how we used to get guys out of bed in the army, kiddo?"

"No."

"Wanna know?"

"No!"

"You got ten seconds to find out . . . nine seconds
to find out . . . eight . . . seven . . . you know what,
Ev? This is fun! . . . Five . . . four . . ."

When he reached zero Abe seized Danny's covers and
jerked all of them off the bed, leaving him lying there
unprotected, shivering.

"Abe, he doesn't sleep with any clothes on."

"Look how much hair he's got on his body now.
Looks just like his old teddy bear. Hey, kiddo, remember Teddy?!"

"What would you like, sweetheart? Juice? Coffee?"

"Uh . . . privacy?"

The shower woke Danny up a little. So did the
shave. The sight of blood, particularly his own, always roused him. He doused himself in Sea Breeze
when he was done, then tried to figure out what to
wear.

Shopping for his new wardrobe had not been a pretty
experience. Abe had taken him to Malibu Clothiers
in Beverly Hills, the place where he said all the "sharp
young guys" bought their "threads." Danny hated
everything in the store. The lapels were too wide. The
bell-bottoms made him look like Captain Kangaroo.
The synthetic material made his skin feel slimy. He and
Abe quarreled. Abe handed him his credit card and
told him to shop for his goddamned self. Danny headed
for Westwood Village and found his old neighborhood had changed. It had been a sleepy, isolated little
UCLA college town when he was a kid. Now it was
the city's center for first-run movies. There were eight
or ten giant new theaters—one of which was shaped
just like a whale. There were restaurants and office
buildings and chain stores, including a two-story Pier
West where Abe's old stationery shop had been. Vaughan
at Sater Gate, the Ivy League men's store, was still
there. Here Danny bought a fine-wale cotton corduroy
suit of a traditional cut that the salesman agreed favored

his *substantial* build. He also bought a suit in khaki and
one in olive, as well as a navy blazer and several pairs
of khaki slacks with straight legs and cuffs. For shirts
he bought oxford button-downs, for ties solid knits
and silk rep stripes. He also bought a pair of dirty bucks
with thick red rubber soles and Bass Weejun penny
loafers.

He chose the khaki suit for his first day on the job,
with a blue shirt and burgundy knit tie. He couldn't
remember how to tie the tie. Abe had to stand behind
him in the mirror, work it over, under, around and
through for him, just like old times.

"Got it now, kiddo?"

"Yeah, it's coming back."

Abe looked him up and down.

"What do you think, Pop?"

"You look like a real square. I like your new wristwatch, though."

Downstairs Danny poured himself coffee.

"Can I get you something to eat, sweetheart?" Ev
wore her robe and slippers and curlers the size of beer
cans.

"No thanks, Mom. Too early for solid food."

He went out back to be by himself, though Coco
insisted on coming with him. It was getting light out
now. The canyon below was still damp and cool and
quiet. Way out, haze was forming over the city.
Danny sipped his coffee. He was fully awake now and
was, he realized, terrified. Not of the new job, but
of *it*.

They took the Cadillac. Abe turned on the air con-
ditioning as soon as they got on the San Diego Freeway, and shut the power windows. It was a silent,
comfortable ride. No one was on the road yet.

"Some kind of crazy car, huh?" grinned Abe, who
drove hunched over the wheel, his chin nearly resting on its rim.

"Crazy," agreed Danny. Briefly he considered push-

ing Abe out and taking it right on down to Mexico.
But that would not, he figured, constitute getting off
on the right foot. "So what will I be, again?"

"Associate chief of personnel."

"And who's the chief?"

"Mom, but I'm phasing her out. Time for her to
relax. She wants to help out at the library over at
the Jewish Community Center, for some reason. What
the hell, she's earned it. She's no kid. I'm starting
you in personnel because I want you to learn the people side of the operation. That's lesson number one—
people are the most important element of any business.
You put in two years there, two years in purchasing, and you'll be ready to be by my side. When I'm
ready to retire, you'll be ready to—"

"Hold it. I only agreed to do this for one year."

"I know. And you can leave any time, but I don't
think you will. Pier West's a big operation now.
We got five-hundred-fifty employees. You have too
much of an interest to just walk away from it.
Don't forget, half of it's yours ever since you turned
twenty-one."

"I haven't forgotten." Danny glanced over at him.
"I can remember when it was just you and mom."

"So can I, kiddo. So can I."

It was called Moss Stationery then. Ev's father, Hap
Moss, had started it. For years Danny had listened
as Abe came forward with one idea after another for
expanding the little shop into a mercantile empire.
Books. Televisions. Art supplies. He had bounced his
ideas off Danny. For some strange reason, he valued
Danny's business opinion. Finally, when Danny was
fourteen, Abe hit on something genuinely new—
inexpensive art prints and home furnishing imports.
Things like Indian bedspreads and candles and wicker
baskets and W.C. Fields posters. Things that would
make a drab UCLA dorm room or student apartment a little homier without costing much. It took off.

Moss Stationery became Pier West. Now there were stores up and down the West Coast with headquarters in La Mirada, where space was cheap.

"Pop?"

"Yo, kiddo?"

"How come you haven't asked where I've been?"

"Figured you'd tell me if you wanted to. Don't forget, I took off from home, too. I know what it's like. Only difference is I never went back."

"I visited your old neighborhood."

"You were in Brooklyn?"

"I was in Bed-Stuy."

"What the hell were you doing there?"

"Just thought I'd take a look."

"How was it?"

"Not great."

"Wasn't great thirty-five years ago. Maybe now you can understand why I came out here. Here, it's new. Clean. There's *room*."

They neared downtown Los Angeles. The Pasadena Freeway interchange lay just ahead. So did traffic. Danny's neck began to itch under his collar.

"Lesson number two," declared Abe. "Ninety-five percent of the people in this world don't know what the hell they're doing. That's why I kept your old lady around for so many years. And why I want you around. Most people are idiots. That's true in all fields, even medicine. You ever need to get cut open, make sure you find one of the five percent who know where to slice."

"If what you say is true—"

"It's true," Abe assured him.

"Then why don't ninety-five percent of the airplanes fall out of the sky?"

"Because there's a God."

"I don't believe in God."

"Then I wouldn't fly, if I were you."

The traffic came to a bumper-to-bumper dead stop

at the spot where the Santa Monica, Santa Ana, Po-
mona, and Golden State Freeways all met. Here there
were smokestacks from the rubber and chemical plants
and five lanes of workers going nowhere in every direction. Bosses. Secretaries. Factory hands. Thousands and thousands of them stuck here. No moving
forward. No turning back. Surrounded.

"This used to be nothing but dairy farms when I first
moved out here," Abe observed. "You could smell
'em for miles. You could also get where you were
going."

"Did God invent traffic?"

"No, we did that."

Danny squirmed impatiently in the seat. "How do
you stand it?"

"Lesson number three," replied Abe. "Don't get upset about things you got no control over. Concentrate on your own *tsuris*. Let Mayor Yorty handle his."

"But he won't handle it unless people like you
force him to. It's up to you to make the noise, to
stand up for the quality of your life. I mean, this is
inhumane."

Abe started laughing.

"What's so funny?" demanded Danny.

"Nothing. I'm not laughing at ya. It's just . . . this
is gonna be fun."

They reached Pier West headquarters in just under
ninety minutes. It was a vast, low, ugly yellow concrete bunker situated next to the freeway in an industrial park of other vast, low, ugly concrete bunkers.
Much of the building was warehouse, with loading
docks around back. There were no cars in the parking lot yet.

"Lesson number four," said Abe, as he unlocked the
front door. "The boss always gets in first." He
handed Danny a key. "This one's yours."

There was a small, unadorned reception area—one
desk, one sofa, two doors. Danny followed Abe

through one of them and down a short, cement-floored corridor. There were several glassed-in offices, then the mailroom, then the supply room, then the warehouse, which was so huge Danny couldn't see to the other end of it.

"Just imagine it as the back room of Moss Stationery," said Abe, "only a thousand times bigger and a million times more *fatumult*. We got the stock, the handling, and the shipping all here under one roof."

"Pop, I probably don't need to say this, but I want to be treated just like any other employee."

"Sorry, kiddo. Can't accommodate you. On you I'll be tougher."

"*That* I'm used to."

A side door led into the general offices, which weren't much more luxurious than where they'd just been, though the floor was carpeted. There was a long gallery with glass-walled offices running along one side. The secretaries' desks were right outside them. Danny followed as Abe rattled off the names of departments.

"Accounting . . . Purchasing . . . Marketing . . . Advertising . . . Personnel, associate chief of."

Danny's office was about halfway down the hall. A pale young woman was stowing her purse in the desk outside of it.

"Ah, good," said Abe. "Pip's here."

She looked up, frightened, at the sound of Abe's voice.

"Pip," Abe said, "meet the new Mister Levine."

Pip was short, thin, and drably dressed. Her eyes were squinty behind thick glasses. "Very glad to know you, Mr. Levine," she said to Danny, offering her hand timidly.

Danny shook it. It was wet. "Likewise."

"Pip's your secretary," Abe explained.

"I have a secretary?" asked Danny, surprised. "Next I'll need a briefcase."

"Got one at home you can have. Nice leather one, not plastic like this. Get settled. We'll talk later."

"I'll drop by."

"No, you won't. We got a chain of command here. Where do you think you are, *home*?" Abe took off down the corridor, hunched over, laughing again.

Danny's office was freshly painted. There was a huge formica-topped desk, high-backed black vinyl swivel chair, and a window that afforded a fine view of the cars stacked up on the Santa Ana Freeway. On one wall was a framed, mounted map of the West Coast of the United States dotted with multicolored stick pins.

He stood there, taking it in. Then he turned around and yelped—Pip was standing right there behind him.

"Sorry, Mr. Levine. I-I didn't mean to startle you."

"That's okay. And call me Danny."

"Oh," she said uncomfortably, eyeing the carpet at her feet.

He circled his desk warily.

"Can I get you some coffee?" Pip offered.

"I don't want to be any bother."

"It's no trouble."

"Just point me to the pot."

"No, really."

"I can—"

"It's my *job*," she blurted out.

He frowned. "Getting me coffee?"

She cleared her throat. "Partly."

"What else do you do?"

"Place calls for you. Pick up. Type. File. And I'm to assist you in any other way I can."

"Well, I hope you'll be patient with me. I've never exactly had a secretary before. How long have you been here?"

"Two years. And I'm very pleased to be working with you. It's a real opportunity, I know."

Danny scratched his chin thoughtfully, was not pleased to find the tiny piece of pastel pink toilet paper still there from when he'd cut himself shaving. He

rolled it into a tiny ball with his thumb, trying to make
the gesture seem natural. "Swell. Okay, Pip. I *would*
like coffee."

"Cream and sugar?"

"No sugar."

"Right away, Mr. Levine."

"Danny."

She scurried off.

Danny sized up the desk again, went around it,
placed both hands palm down on it, and slowly eased
himself down into the big chair. He placed his elbows
on the desk and made a steeple of his fingers. He
opened the middle drawer: pens, pencils, erasers, paper clips, bottle of Excedrin. All new, all neatly arranged. He closed the middle drawer. He reached for
the phone, picked it up, held it to his ear, put it back
down, moved it a little closer to him. He took a deep
breath, let it out slowly. Then he finally sat all the
way back in the swivel chair.

It backflipped him. Threw him head-over-heels onto
the rug behind his desk. His head and shoulders ended
up wedged against the wall while his feet flailed in
space. Dazed, he toppled over to one side, raised himself on one elbow, and discovered a pair of female legs
standing in his doorway. He scampered sheepishly
to his feet and righted the chair.

She was a willowy, nice-looking young woman, a
Chicano, with creamy skin, glossy black hair, and
dark brown eyes. She was wearing a black dress. She
had a very nice smile. Her teeth were white.

"Mr. Levine?" she inquired.

"Danny. Yeah." She was *real* pretty. He began to
play with his tie.

"I'm Doris Valenca. I'm very pleased to meet you."

"G-great. Where do you work?"

"Right now I'm in purchasing. I just wanted to welcome you, and tell you if there's anything I can do,
just ask. I know I'm not your secretary, but we don't

believe in formal breakdowns here. I'm here to help.
Advice. Anything."

"That's real nice of you."

"I love your tie. It goes with your eyes."

Danny stopped fiddling with it, shoved his hands in
his pockets. "Gee, thanks. And thanks for stopping
by. Purchasing, right?"

"*Doris.*"

Pip appeared in the doorway with a steaming Pier
West mug that had "Danny" printed on it. She scowled
at Doris. "Excuse me," she said coldly as she pressed
past her.

Doris flared her nostrils at Pip, then wiggled her fingers at Danny and sashayed out on high heels, twitch-
ing her tail like a prized palomino. It was some tail.
Danny found himself staring after her.

When he turned back to Pip she was glowering at
him.

"She seems nice," he said.

"She's a cheap, conniving slut." Pip put his coffee
on his desk, spun on her heel, and sped out.

"Pip?" he called after her, shocked.

She didn't answer him. He heard her sit at her desk
outside his door.

"Pip?!" he called again, louder this time.

The phone on his desk buzzed. The phone had several buttons on it. One of them was blinking on and
off. He punched it tentatively and picked up the phone.

"Uh . . . hello?"

"Mr. Levine?"

"Yes. This is *Danny* Levine."

"This is Pip. If you want me, buzz me."

"How do I—?"

"The intercom button."

"Oh."

She hung up. He buzzed her.

"Yes, Mr. Levine?"

"What did you mean . . . about Doris?"

"I meant she wanted my job and still wants it."

"How come?"

"Are you settled in?"

"I suppose. Why?"

"I'm supposed to introduce you around."

"Isn't my . . . I mean, I figured—"

"He asked me to do it. More diplomatic that way. Take off your jacket. Mr. Levine likes a shirtsleeve approach."

"Should I roll up my sleeves?"

"I would."

There were about two dozen management-type people in the Pier West front office, and nearly all of them were gray. Gray complexions. Gray hair. Gray personalities. They looked as if they seldom smiled, though they were smiling now. They were trying hard to make the new personnel, associate chief of, feel good and welcome. They stopped conversations midsentence to make him feel welcome. They pumped his hand, patted his shoulder, told him how happy they were to "have him aboard." They all seemed to use that expression, as if headquarters were located somewhere in the North Atlantic.

"They're trying to be hearty," Pip explained matter-of-factly when he asked her about it.

There were two people who weren't gray. One was Larry Borok, the accountant. Larry was green. Lime green polyester, to be exact, with festive ecru stitching, matching lime green tie, and shiny yellow shirt. Larry was in his late twenties, and blinked a lot. He was very wound up.

"Yes, yes?" he demanded impatiently, as Danny and Pip stood in the doorway to his office.

"Mr. Borok, this is Danny Levine," said Pip. "Our new personnel associate."

"Fine. Hello."

Larry stood and extended a hand across his desk. He was tall and gawky and listed slightly to one side.

There was a serious dandruff problem. The word goon came to mind. Danny shook his hand.

Then Larry sat back down, lit a Kent, and returned to his papers. He glanced up a second later, surprised and annoyed that Danny and Pip were still there.

"Sorry. Rather busy," he said, dismissing them.

"Larry needs work on his people skills," Pip confided as they proceeded down the corridor.

Irv Green in marketing wasn't gray either. He was black. Irv was in his early thirties. He had a neatly-trimmed Afro and a full beard and wore a blue workshirt with a striped tie, rumpled Levi cords, and Wallabees. The eyes behind his wire-rimmed glasses were lively and amused. Plants grew in his office. A couple of Pier West posters—one of the Grateful Dead, one of the Marx Brothers—adorned his walls. An Indian bedspread covered the black vinyl loveseat.

Danny immediately felt at home in Irv's office. Irv's hand was dry and firm.

"Welcome," Irv said warmly. "Glad to see a young face."

"Likewise," Danny agreed. "Not too many here."

"Nope. Meet Larry?"

Danny nodded.

"He's an okay lad, once you get to know him. A little hyper, but okay. Your dad calls us his Young Turks. Now there's three of us. You jog?"

Danny patted his belly. "Not hardly."

"I do three miles every day, right here alongside the freeway."

"Shouldn't you wear a gas mask?"

"I do," Irv replied, producing a NASA-style face mask from his desk. "Filters out the carbon monoxide. Care to join me?"

"I'll give it some thought."

"Do that. We'll have to get together for lunch. Rap."

Danny tried not to grimace, but failed.

Irv grinned. "Sorry. Force of habit. I talk like that

to tick off the various old people. Will you eat lunch
with me if I promise not to use that word again?"

Danny laughed. "I won't if you won't."

"Deal. Look forward to it."

Pip didn't introduce Danny to the secretaries, but he
noticed he was being checked out by the young ones.
Some of them were cute, though not as nice looking
as Doris.

Pip led him through the reception area to the shipping department and then to the warehouse, where
he met the husky young warehouse manager, Bobby
Clarke. The warehouse floor was hopping now. Rock
music blared. Guys moved crates around on forklifts,
loading and unloading trucks. Many of them were
long hairs, and they whooped and laughed while they
worked. They seemed to be having a lot more fun
than the gray people. Oddly, no one seemed to notice
him as he stood there with Pip and Bobby.

He was management.

He decided he needed another cup of coffee when
he and Pip got back to his office. He grabbed his cup
and started past Pip's desk with it.

"Mr. Levine . . ." she called after him.

"I really don't like being waited on," he told her
firmly. "I'll get it myself."

She sighed. "Very well."

"Where is it?"

"Around the corner. Past the Xerox machine."

As he headed into the coffee room, silent on his
rubber-soled bucks, he heard female voices coming
from inside, chattering on top of each other:

"Can you *believe* she got the job?"

"She's such a little—"

"And she thinks she's so smart now—"

"He's not even bad looking—"

"Is he married?"

"I don't—"

Danny coughed.

It was three of the young secretaries, two chubby, one plain. Their eyes widened when they saw him. Frozen grins followed.

"Mr. Levine. Hi."

"Hi, Mr. Levine."

"Hullo," he said.

They stood there in mortified silence while he poured his coffee. When he left, he heard gasps and giggles behind him.

"Pip?" he said sharply as he strode past her desk.

"Yes?"

"From now on you can get my coffee."

"Very well. Mr. Levine wants to know if you're free for lunch."

"I am."

"He'll meet you at the car."

They ate nearby at a big cafeteria called Arnold's Farmhouse. Danny had fish sticks, tater tots, and creamed corn. Abe had Jell-O, cottage cheese, and a cup of plain hot water.

"How you like it so far, kiddo?"

"It's a little dizzying."

"Relax. You got time. Meet my Young Turks?"

"Uh-huh."

"Irving and Larry are my boys. Handpicked 'em."

"I feel . . . conspicuous."

"You're the heir. People are gonna watch you, size you up. It's natural. Just be yourself. You probably ought to join the bowling team. I never could, on account of my back."

"I don't bowl."

"It's good p.r. . . . Have a pizza with them, some laughs. Just remember to pick up the tab. Pip okay?"

Danny nodded. "There seems to be some resentment from the others."

"That's natural, too. If you like her, she'll move up with you, become one of the most powerful people in the company. Bound to be some jealousy. That reminds me, some of the those girls are pretty sharp looking."

"Doris is—"

"Stay away from 'em. Only jerks and losers fool around with the secretaries. Can't stand guys who walk around the office with their dick in their hand. As bad as drunks. I know you're a healthy young stud—"

"Healthy young stud?"

"But get your action somewhere else. That's lesson number . . . what number are we on?"

"I lost count. Is that why you gave me Pip?"

"Whattya mean?"

"She is far and away the homeliest woman in the company."

"She's the *smartest*. And she doesn't gossip. You seeing anybody these days?"

"I just got back in town, Pop."

"You'll be wanting your own pad, I guess."

"There's time."

"I see. Don't want to commit yourself, huh?" Danny shrugged. "I don't know what I can afford."

"You can afford anything you want."

"But isn't your rent supposed to be based on your salary?"

"Yeah."

"So what's my salary?"

"How much do you think it should be?"

"Are you negotiating with me?"

"When you're head of personnel you'll go through this with every employee." Abe sipped at his hot water. "What did you make on your last job?"

"Two dollars a bushel."

"Hmm."

"What does Pip make?"

"One-fifty."

"An hour?"

"A week. I'll start you at three hundred. Minus two weeks salary, of course."

"For what?" Danny demanded.

"Your threads."

"Oh, right. To do what?"

"Your job. That's all I ask, kiddo."

"But what *is* my job?"

"I want you to learn the organization. See how the manpower is dispersed. Visit the stores. See how they're staffed. Then I want you to come up with answers."

"Answers to what?"

"What our biggest personnel problems are and how we can lick 'em."

"Wouldn't you be better off with . . . I mean, aren't there people who actually have degrees in that sort of thing?"

"I don't want some jerk with a slide rule. I want you. Your fresh eye. Your input. Talk to the department heads. Take 'em to lunch. Find out what's on their minds. Talk to the store managers. They're out there in the field. They see things, hear things. Put it all down on paper. Assemble a report for me. I want answers. I want bold ideas. We didn't come this far in ten years by going with the efficiency experts. Understand?"

"I think so. Can you give me some idea of what I'm looking for?"

"No. I don't want to influence you. Take as much time as you need. First of August will be fine."

"That's less than—"

"So get cracking, kiddo. Think I'm paying you big bucks to sit around and eat lunch?"

Chapter Five

"Here, Pip. Grab the other end, would you?"

Danny stood on a chair in front of his office window, holding up a Pier West roll-up bamboo shade. He had already put out a tatami-style area rug and experimented with scented candles. The candles hadn't been a success. For one thing, they smelled like peach-scented poison gas. For another, when Danny blew them out the smoke had triggered the building's automatic sprinkler system and doused every employee in the Pier West front office.

Already the big fella was making his presence felt.

Pip brought a chair around, stood on it, and hoisted the other end of the shade. "Why are you putting this up?"

"So I won't have to keep staring at the freeway."

"But your back is to the window."

"I still know it's there."

She shook her head. "I must tell you, Danny. I've never worked for anyone quite like you."

"Gee, sorry."

"No. Don't be." She flushed slightly, looked away. "I like it, I think."

It was Friday, the end of his first week, and this was their first warm encounter. The working rapport was there. Pip was efficient, quick, helpful, and didn't seem to mind working for someone who was clearly a bozo. True, she hadn't smiled yet. Not once. But she was incredibly valuable.

"Does it look even to you?" Danny asked her.

"Higher on your side."

It was her idea to drop in on the stores unannounced and thereby get a better idea of how they worked. She'd laid a map out on his desk and shown him where to go. So far he'd visited the Pier Wests in Alameda, Arcadia, Alhambra, Altadena, Alta Loma, Anaheim, Artesia, and Azusa. Monday he got to go to Bell-flower. The stores were very much alike. The main thing Danny noticed was how little merchandise they carried that he'd actually buy for himself. He personally liked old things, the kind of furniture and lamps and cups and saucers they used in 1930s black-and-white movies. There was something solid and comfort-about that stuff. Not that Pier West was in the business of selling used things, but why not reproductions? This was something worth keeping in mind, maybe talking to Irv about. Irv seemed like a real good guy. A Grate-ful Deadhead even. Have to get to know him better.

Pip had also prepared thumbnail sketches of each of the department heads and set up his interviews for him. After each one he'd dictate his notes into a small tape recorder. She'd transcribe them, organize them, and convert them to precise, grown-up sounding language, language that somehow made them seem even more lame.

There was no point in kidding himself—Danny was getting absolutely nowhere with this, his first as-signment as personnel, associate chief of.

"Pip, how come nobody will tell me what's wrong with this place?"

"Fear," she replied in her matter-of-fact way.

"Fear of what?"

"That it might get back to your father."

"I'm starting to feel like some kind of snitch. There," he said, adjusting the shade. "Is it even now?"

"I believe so."

Danny picked up the hammer and drove a hook into the wall, along with his thumb and index finger. He yelped.

"Here, trade with me," Pip ordered.

She took over measuring, marking, tapping. She was good at that kind of thing. She even knew how to fold a map.

"Not very handy, are you?" she said.

"No, I'm not. My pop always wanted me to be the kind of person who hired someone else to do that kind of work for him. Someone with dirty finger-nails. He can't stand the way mine look now." Danny held up his gnarled, blackened, peach-picker's hands and was astonished to see that in just a few short days they'd already gone back to their smooth, pink, natural state.

"There," she said, hopping down off the chair. "All done."

"Thanks, Pip," he said.

"You're welcome," she said, almost but not quite smiling.

It was starting to bother him. "Pip, are you happy?"

"With my job, you mean?"

"With life in general."

She shrugged. "Who is?"

"Nobody?" he suggested.

"Nobody I know."

"Think about it much?"

"What for?"

"Thanks again."

"You're welcome," she said, puzzled, on her way out.

Danny sighed, lowered his new shade, and sat, very

carefully, in his chair. No telling when it might decide to throw him again.

He looked up to find Art Lubin, the head buyer, standing in his doorway. Art was the grayest of the gray people. Even his teeth were gray.

"Your dad said I should talk to *you* about this situation I have," said Art, a tiny bit skeptically.

"Okay. Sure. Have a seat."

Art stood right where he was, jangling the coins in his pocket. "I'd like your . . . the company's authorization to let Nate Birnbaum go."

"Uncle Natey?"

Nate Birnbaum used to peddle greeting cards to Abe at Moss Stationery. He was a sweet little guy, a widower, an old-time *shlepper*. Also a regular visitor to the old house when Grandpa was still alive. He always came armed with a chocolate sucker from See's Candy for Danny and a couple of jokes with Yiddish punchlines that would make Hap laugh. No mean feat this. Generally Danny's grandpa either scowled or barked at the world—that was how he got his nickname, and he got it *before* he went blind. They were seriously dirty, Natey's jokes. Danny knew this because whenever he'd ask Abe for a translation Abe would send him to Westward Ho to buy another jar of mixed nuts. These days Abe used Natey as a phone buyer.

"What's the problem with Natey?"

"He's not pulling his weight," Art replied.

"Pop always said he was a good worker."

"He was, only he just won't put in the hours anymore. He's constantly late getting in in the morning. I've told him he has to get in earlier. I've told him and told him and told him. Here, look . . ." Art stepped forward with a chart, which he laid out on Danny's desk. "I've kept his attendance record for the past month. See this? Nine twenty-three . . . nine thirty-one . . . nine twenty . . ."

It was a lavish chart. Color coded.

"Can't he work a little later to make up for it?" asked Danny.

"He's my East Coast buyer. Three hours later there. When it's five o'clock here they've gone home. By the time he gets here in the morning they've gone to lunch. The only time he can get hold of them is when they're back from lunch, only then *he's* out to lunch." Art shook his head. "It's killing me."

"Hmm." Danny tugged at his ear. "How about switching him to a different territory?"

"I'm not rearranging my entire department to accommodate one man. Everyone else manages to get here on time. That's all I'm asking of Nate. But I'm through asking. It's no use. I've got to go with someone else. Someone young, hungry. Surely *you* can understand that."

Danny reached for the phone and punched the intercom button. "Pip, could you please ask Nate Birnbaum to come in?"

"Right," she replied.

"And . . . please hold all of my calls."

"Yessir."

Art shifted uncomfortably from one foot to the other.

"You don't mind, do you?" Danny asked him.

"No, no," Art replied quickly. He sat.

"How old is Natey now?" Danny asked him while they waited.

"Sixty-two."

He looked older. Also browbeaten and weary and, when he spotted Art Lubin sitting there, very worried. Art's eyes avoided his.

"Sit, Natey. Sit," said Danny.

Nate sat, licking his lips nervously. He'd lost some weight. His shirt hung low and loose at the neck. It was not a robust fashion statement.

"How are you feeling, Natey?" Danny asked him, personally feeling very weird about all of this.

"Can't complain. A little trouble with my pressure, but the new medication keeps it down good."

"Your daughter well?"

"Lenore's very well, thanks. She's living in Orlando now. Has two lovely boys. Her husband's a school superintendant. I take my vacation with them every winter."

"Good. Glad to hear it." Danny cleared his throat. "The reason I asked you in, Natey, is that Art here says he's having some problems with your hours."

Nate glanced over at Art and reddened. "I-I try to get in on time, Danny. I really do. It's the traffic, see? Can't handle it no more. Gives me the shakes. I-I leave a little later, I stay a little later. Not such a big *geshrai*, is it?"

"Actually," Danny countered gently, "it sounds like it *is* a pretty big thing if it's cutting into the hours you can work the phone. Let me ask you something— have you ever thought about leaving the house really early, so you can beat some of the traffic? That's what Pop and I do. You could get a lot of your calls in before they leave for lunch."

Nate glanced over at Art again. This time Art reddened.

"I volunteered to do that," Nate said. "Only Mr. Lubin here, he said . . ."

"I said no," Art declared, bristling.

"Why?" Danny asked him.

"Because I like to stay on top of things in my department. He'd be unsupervised if he was here that early."

Danny frowned. "You mean, you're afraid he'd be goofing off?"

"Well, not in so many—"

"This is Nate Birnbaum," Danny pointed out. "He's a pro. You don't have to worry about—"

"Young man, are you telling me how to run things in my—"

"No. I'm trying to find a solution here. I think maybe there is one. At least it's worth a try." Danny turned back to Nate, who now appeared to be sitting a little taller in his chair. "Tell you what, Natey . . ." Danny removed the front door key from his keychain, held it out to him across the desk. "Have Pip make you a copy of this. That way you can let yourself in if Pop and I aren't here yet. That okay?"

"That's plenty okay," exclaimed Nate, taking it. He started for the door.

"There's only one thing, Natey," Danny cautioned him.

"Oh, you don't have to worry about me, Danny boy. I'll be here at seven on the dot."

"That's not what I meant. You have to start the coffee."

Nate laughed. "For you, young fella, I'll grind the beans." Then he left.

Danny turned back to Art, who was not pleased, and said, "I really don't think you'll have any more problems with him. But if you do, let me know. Then we'll consider the next step."

"Very well, Mr. Levine," Art said curtly.

Danny watched him leave, reflecting that Art was one person he didn't mind calling him Mr. Levine.

A moment later Pip came back in and sat down primly in the chair opposite him. She had business to discuss.

He placed his elbows on his desk and made a steeple of his fingers. "Yes?"

"Irv and Larry want to have lunch with you today."

"Sounds good."

She cleared her throat uneasily. "I told them they could confide in you."

"Good."

"Are you sure?" she pressed.

"Of course I'm sure. I . . . Wait, what exactly do you mean by 'confide in me'?"

"You won't repeat what they say to your father."

"I'm supposed to tell my father what I find out."

"You don't necessarily have to tell him where you heard it."

"That's true," he admitted.

"I promised them you wouldn't."

"Oh?"

"They're bright and they care. They can help you."

Danny tugged at his ear. Something was happening here. Possibly his first break. "Okay, Pip. It's a deal."

Danny and the Turks ate at Arnold's. Danny had Jell-O and cottage cheese. Irv had tuna salad. Larry picked at his meat loaf platter and chain-smoked Kents while he ate. He wore his cocoa brown polyester ensemble today.

"Your dad said you've been traveling," Irv said.

Danny grinned. "Yeah, that's one word for it."

"What's another?" asked Larry, frowning.

"Must have had some great experiences," said Irv, stroking his beard fondly. "I sure did."

"You bummed around?" Danny asked him.

"Before I started business school. Rode a bike through Greece for a year. No schedule. No responsibilities. It was great. Never be able to do *that* again."

"Know what you mean," said Danny.

"I've got a wife and baby now. It's hard to imagine ever—"

"So, can we get to the goddamned point?" broke in Larry.

Irv laughed. "Don't mind Larry, Danny. All he thinks about is business. Business and baseball."

"You're a baseball fan?" Danny asked Larry.

Larry nodded grudgingly. "Got season tickets to the Dodgers."

"My pop used to take me to Dodger games," Danny said. "I remember he got real pissed when we lost Cuba. Castro liked to play baseball. To him that meant we could have done business with the guy."

Baseball. Danny hadn't thought about the game in years. Funny, since it was his whole life when he was a kid. Tucked away in his bedroom with his green plastic transistor radio, listening to Vin Scully's voice on KFI from those distant battlefields. Connie Mack Stadium in Philadelphia. Crosley Field in Cincinnati, with its terraced warning track. Sitting there on his bed, surrounded by his personal legion of cardboard soldiers, brave, square-jawed, smelling of bubble gum. Vada Pinson. Milt Pappas. Virgil Trucks. Minnie Minoso. Julian Javier. *Baseball.*

"Like to go some time?" Larry asked him uncomfortably.

"Gee, it's been years. I . . . Actually, I wouldn't mind. Stadium still nice?"

"It's the team that sucks cock. New kids aren't ready. That Garvey can't throw the ball from—"

"So can we talk business?" broke in Irv, kidding.

"Fuck off, Green," snapped Larry testily.

"I'm supposed to try to get an idea of where the company is at—what's wrong with it from a personnel point of view," Danny said. "I've been talking to different people. Hearing their ideas."

They nodded noncommittally.

"Having any luck?" asked Irv.

"No," he confessed.

"Too bad," said Irv. "I'm not really surprised, though. It's a pretty uptight bunch. Most of them were hired when Pier West was still a mom and pop outfit."

"Glorified bookkeepers," sniffed Larry.

"No need to get nasty about it," pointed out Irv.

"It's a *fact*," insisted Larry.

"That's what I want," said Danny. "Facts."

"Facts," repeated Irv. "Okay. The fact is Pier West has grown dramatically over the past three years. It's a very exciting time for the company. We're poised

right on the brink of becoming a major national retail chain."

"Or not," countered Larry.

"Or not," agreed Irv. "The next couple of years are
crucial."

"Can you give me an idea where the trouble spots
are?" Danny asked.

Irv and Larry exchanged a look.

"Seriously?" asked Larry.

"Yes. And you guys have my word—what's said
here at this table stays here, at least the source does."

Irv and Larry exchanged another look and a nod.

"Okay," said Irv. "We're going to lay something
on you, Danny. Something heavy. Something that
has to be dealt with or . . ."

"Or we're going to have to leave the company,"
Larry said.

"I see," said Danny. "Go ahead."

Irv leaned forward slightly. "The major trouble spot
with Pier West is your father."

Chapter Six

The Sterns and Waldmans gave Mouse and Wendy a three-bedroom ranch-style home with a swimming pool on a cul-de-sac in Sherman Oaks. It was 107 degrees out there when Danny drove over the hill— fifteen degrees hotter than the West Side. It was always fifteen degrees hotter out in the Valley.

Mouse and a blast of frosty, air-conditioned air greeted Danny at the door. Mouse wore only gurkha shorts, a pith helmet, and some white stuff on his nose. He was as bony as ever. Wendy wore a string bikini, a mezuzah, and a great deal of oil.

To Danny's surprise, the house was already totally furnished, as if they'd been living there for years instead of days. The living room and dining area were done in white wicker with pale green cushions. There were many potted plants.

"Hunh?!" exclaimed Mouse, arms out expansively. "Hunh?"

"Gee, this looks like a place where grownups live," observed Danny.

They stared at him blankly.

"We *are* grownups, Levine," Mouse said.

"I know. I mean, it's very nice."

Mouse's study featured a clear Lucite desk that was bare save for two telephones and the plastic vomit from his stag party.

The master bedroom had black walls and black carpeting. The king-sized bed was on a pedestal and was covered by a shiny red and black bedspread.

"Sometimes we don't come outta here for days, if you read me," Mouse said with a wink.

"Mickey!"

"Wanna see her underwear drawer, Levine?"

"Mickey-wickey! You're being bad!"

"Aw, I *asked* you not to call me that in front of my friends," whined Mouse. "Too early for a beer, Levine?"

"Never too early for a beer. Just point me to the—"

"Nonsense, you're our guest. Cookie, go get him a beer."

She padded off toward the kitchen, her greased flanks wiggling.

Mouse ogled her, then winked again at Danny. "The truth, Levine. Ever think you'd see me settled down this way?"

"The truth? No."

"Go on," laughed Mouse.

"Great place, Stern."

"Designer did all of it. Only trouble is the *where.* There was a fucking tumbleweed in our yard this morning. I mean, do I look like Hopalong Cassidy to you?"

"No, you don't," Danny replied. "It's only five minutes over the hill from the West Side."

"It's like Siberia, only hot. Fuck it—we'll make it back in a year. Or die trying." Mouse snatched a look at his watch. "Rachel may come," he said off-handedly. "We try to stay in touch. You don't mind, do you?"

Danny shrugged. "No, I don't mind."

The pool was small and kidney-shaped. Lox, cream

cheese, and fruit salad were out there sweating on a table in the shade. Some of that syrupy new California zen rock that Danny didn't like was coming out of the outdoor speakers. Jackson Browne was the singer.

Danny pulled off his T-shirt and flopped down in his swimming trunks on a lounge chair. Mouse joined him, lit a joint, and handed it over. Danny drew deeply on it.

"So, how's business?" Mouse asked like an old Jew.

Danny closed his eyes and sighed like an old Jew. "Don't ask."

And he meant it. Irv and Larry had given him a whole file detailing just how Abe was screwing up Pier West. The problem, it seemed, was that nothing could be done without Abe's personal approval. He didn't delegate authority, didn't trust anyone, wouldn't take advice, wouldn't look ahead. This made for serious logjams and even more serious errors in judgment. He refused to start manufacturing his own merchandise, even though he was having to buy it at higher and higher prices—and shave his profit margin. He turned down a major new line of garden furniture from Taiwan that North Country Fair was now cleaning up on. He also said no to the cheap gauze clothing from India. Import Barn was now doing well enough with it for Pier West to feel the pinch. Morale was low. Top young people weren't staying. Turnover and pilfering at the outlets were alarmingly high, in large part because employee wages and benefits were well below the other chains. Irv and Larry were armed with facts, figures, ideas. Pip was right. They really seemed to care about the company. If only Danny did, but he didn't.

"Here, Danny."

Wendy stood over him with a tray. A cold Tuborg, two white wines, and her breasts were on it. Straining against the white bikini. He reached for the beer. Mouse took a glass of white wine. She sat down.

"So all of this is yours," said Danny.

"All mine," agreed Mouse. "I mean, *ours*."

"Hey, how was the honeymoon? I got your card."

Wendy looked at the pool. "Okay."

"We came back early," explained Mouse. "A lot we wanted to get done here."

"Well, it certainly was worth it."

"Did you tell him Rachel may come?" Wendy asked Mouse.

"I could have given her a ride," said Danny. "If I'd known."

"She wasn't sure she could make it," said Mouse. "What the hell, if I try to pressure her, she doesn't come. She's contrary."

The doorbell rang.

"That'll be her," said Mouse. *"Maybe."*

Wendy went to answer it.

"Seriously, Levine. Job okay?"

"I guess. It seems like all I do now is work. Last night I actually fell asleep in front of the TV. Me and Pop. My mom said she wanted to take a picture, only she was out of film."

"That's why it's so important to love your work. Work is all there is, if you happen to be a Hebraic male. So why haven't you called my gorgeous, unattached sister? I'll bet she's a great lay. All that anger."

"That's no way to talk about your own sister."

"I apologize. Sometimes I get vulgar. It's from hanging around with movie people."

"No it isn't. You were always vulgar. Look, neither of us is into dating right now, okay?"

"Don't you like her?" pressed Mouse.

"She's *fine*. Just forget it. She wouldn't be interested in me anyway."

"She told me she thinks you're still the sweetest guy in the world."

"She did? Gee . . . How did that happen to come up?"

"I asked."

Rachel was wearing a tank top and gym shorts. Her hair was brushed loose, and her sunglasses were perched on her head. For a second, from across the patio, she still looked like Malibu Rachel. But then she came a little closer, and she was Rachel with the sunken eyes.

"Michael, I love what you did to the house," she called to him. "It's *beautiful*."

"Thanks, Sis."

"Mickey-wickey?!" yelled Wendy from inside. "Come help me cut the bagels!"

"I asked you *not* to call me that!" he yelled back. Then he got up, muttering to himself, and headed in.

Rachel sat down in a chair next to Danny and stripped off her tank top. She was wearing a bikini top underneath and showing several more ribs than she had. Clearly, she was not getting proper nourishment.

Danny offered her the joint. She shook her head.

"Nice place, huh?" he said.

"If I had to live here I'd burn it to the ground," she shot back.

"It's not my taste," he acknowledged.

"It's *no* taste."

"How are your pots coming?"

"Okay."

"I'd like to see them some time."

"What for?"

Danny swallowed. "No reason." Stung, he got to his feet, pulled in his stomach, and gallumphed over to the diving board. So much for being the sweetest guy in the world.

The board had super spring to it. It sailed him higher than he expected and threw off his Tacaloma Swim School Sinker's Grade Acapulco cliff dive just enough so that he sliced through the water's surface more like an airborne baby whale than a steak knife. The water was soft and too warm to be refreshing. He surfaced.

Rachel sat on the edge now, paddling in the water with her bare feet. Her pearly toenails glistened in the bright, hot sun.

"I'm sorry, Danny," she said. "I didn't mean to bite your head off. It's this place. It's *them*."

He nodded, slumped down onto the steps next to her in the shallow end.

"I don't know why they freak me out like they do," she said. "I guess it's because they're so . . ."

"Real?" he suggested.

"Fake."

Danny nodded again.

"How's your work?" she asked.

"You really interested?"

"I asked, didn't I?"

"It's okay. Only, it doesn't matter. It's just soap dishes and throw pillows and profit and loss statements. It's not me."

"Is that so important?"

"It's everything. If work isn't meaningful, if we just put in time, do a job, then that makes us just like everybody else. And we're not."

So true. Who else could say they'd actually been yelled at by Mister Ed?

"I'm glad to hear you say that," she said, warming to him.

"You are?"

Mouse started outside with a bowl of bagels. When he saw they were deep in conversation he spun on his heel and went back inside.

"It doesn't matter to a lot of people anymore," she said, eyeing the back door. "What exactly are you doing?"

"I'm in personnel. There's actually five hundred and fifty employees now. I'm supposed to find out what the biggest problems are with them and come up with recommendations."

"I think that could be very exciting."

"You do?" he said, surprised and intrigued. "How?"

"By not thinking about the company."

"But that's my job."

"Not necessarily. Think about the five hundred and fifty people. Think about what would make their lives more productive, more fulfilling. This could be a really meaningful opportunity for you, Danny. You could help make Pier West the model of a modern, socially responsible corporation. You could bring it into the seventies."

"I really haven't thought about it that way. I've been concentrating more on the business itself."

"It's the people who matter."

"Right," he agreed. "You know, you may be on to something there. The *people*. I'm gonna have to give that some more thought. How'd you get to be so smart?"

"I watched a lot of TV as a child. And I had you as a friend. Anything else I can help you with?"

"My secretary."

She was amused. "Danny Levine has a secretary."

"And she doesn't like me."

"I find that hard to believe."

"No, really. She never smiles. Ever."

"She's just uptight. Bring her flowers."

"What for?"

"You don't need a what for. Trust me."

Mouse and Wendy came out together with the bagels and more drinks. The four of them ate at the table in the shade. Rachel just nibbled on some fruit salad. Danny quietly slipped a half bagel with cream cheese onto her plate, but she wouldn't touch it. Mouse told some funny stories about famous show business people Danny had never heard of. Rachel didn't join in the laughter.

Mouse lit a small cigar when he had finished eating. Wendy started to clear the table.

"I'll help," offered Danny.

"Levine, there's women here, would ya?"

"Oink, oink," said Rachel.

"I don't mind," said Danny, grabbing some plates.

"Levine, we got a dishwasher. Levine, come back . . . !"

The kitchen was huge and shiny. It looked like a place where they would film a cat food commercial. Danny loaded the dishwasher while Wendy wrapped the leftovers.

"Thanks for helping, Wuggy. You're very considerate."

"No problem."

"Actually, I've been thinking about you. This may sound kind of funny, but I keep thinking we're gonna get back together."

Danny froze, and managed not to drop the wine goblet he was holding. "Y-you're right," he said.

"You're thinking the same thing?"

"No, it sounds kind of funny. Wendy, you just got married."

"That doesn't mean I can't do my thing."

" 'Your thing'?"

"We're not like our parents, Wuggy. Even our parents weren't like our parents, if you can dig where I'm coming from."

"No, I don't think I can, actually."

"I could tell you stories about Daddy the Rabbi—"

"Don't. That's okay."

"Michael and I are different. Our marriage is based on total freedom. I do my thing, he does his. It's all out in the open. That way there's no hypocrisy. It's not the doing that's wrong. It's the hypocrisy."

"So let me see if I've got this right. By 'your thing' you mean . . . ?"

"Sex."

"And this works?"

"So far. Of course, we just started."

"Wendy, why did you get married?"

"I wanted to."

"Why did you marry Mouse?"

"He wanted to."

Danny put the last dish in the washer, closed it, turned and found Wendy blocking his path. She leaned into him, her breasts pressing softly against his bare chest, her skin hot and slick against his. Then she put her arms around his neck and kissed him. She always could kiss. He kissed her right back. Hungrily. It had been a while since he'd had his last woman. It had been a previous decade.

But then his wits returned and he pulled back abruptly, panting.

"What's wrong, Wuggy?" she gasped. "Don't you want me anymore?"

"You know very well that isn't it."

"What then?"

"This isn't *right*."

She smiled. Then she took his hand and kissed it. "You're so old-fashioned."

"I am?"

"If you change your mind, call me, okay? I mean it. I'm so horny I could die."

"Why don't you have sex with your husband?"

"Oh, we don't do that sort of thing."

Danny shook his head. "I don't get it, Little Gal. I'm sorry."

He went back outside. Mouse was floating on a raft in the pool, puffing away contentedly on his cigar. Rachel was sitting in the shade. He joined her.

"I don't know what's happened to the institution of marriage," he fumed. "I really, really don't."

"It turned to shit," she said. "Just like everything else did."

Chapter Seven

"C'mon, Doris!" urged Tommy from shipping. "Get us that spare!"

"Let's go, Dorrie!" called Sandy from sales. "We can take this one!"

Doris was wearing the tightest white pants Danny had ever seen. He got a fine view of her shapely behind when she bent over to retrieve her ball. After she straightened up she looked over her shoulder at Danny and flashed him a smile.

"Go get 'em, Doris!" he yelled, clapping his hands.

Bobby Clarke, the warehouse manager, nudged him. Bobby was a big, red-bearded guy in his early thirties who wore low-slung jeans and a big, shiny Harley Davidson belt buckle. "God, I wish I was falling into *that* tonight," he groaned.

Danny sipped his beer and stifled a yawn. He wasn't enjoying this. He didn't want to be here at the Jim Fregosi Family Funarama in Fullerton, wearing a Pier West All-Stars T-shirt, buying the beers, and acting like a good sport while they got murdered by the team from Bridgestone Tire, which was made up of several very gung-ho middle-aged guys who all seemed to be named Vic.

The folks on the Pier West team were nice enough.
Bobby. Tommy. Doris. Sandy. Phil. Sheila. Ramon,
from the mailroom, who had brought his wife and
seven children. But they were about as dull as Ginger Baker's drum solo on side two of *Blind Faith*. And
he still had a briefcase full of work to do. More of
Pip's transcriptions of his interview notes to be di-
gested and edited by morning. A *Wall Street Journal*
article Irv had passed him, all about a brewery being
started in Northern California by a Maytag heir as a
wholly cooperative venture. A memo from A.L.—
Abe—notifying him—D.L.—that he was being sent
to a week-long personnel management seminar at
Murietta Hot Springs in September. The brochure called
it "indispensable." A.L. called it "so maybe you'll
learn something." A memo from I.G.—Irv—responding
to his own memo about '30s reproductions. "D.L.
—Love the repro idea. Could be hot with we boom-
ers. Try it out on A.L."

Personally Danny wasn't crazy about this initials business, but his personal opinions didn't seem to matter
much these days. Only the job did. There were more
and more demands being placed on him. He didn't
even get to go home after this. Abe thought it was too
long a drive to make so late at night, so Pip had
booked him a room at a Holiday Inn. Danny felt himself getting sucked deeper and deeper into Pier West.
Only his feet were sticking out now, and they were in
bowling shoes.

"Hey, Bobby," he said, glumly. "You happy?"

"Shoot, yeah. Couple brews. A chick. That's what
it's all about, isn't it?"

"Is it?"

"Shoot, yeah. Your pop?"

"Yeah?"

"He's a swell guy."

Doris missed the spare. That left it up to Danny.

"Let's go, Danny boy!" called Phil.

"C'mon, Danno!" cried Sheila.

Danny got sheepishly to his feet and found his ball. He was the only one on the team incapable of breaking a hundred. He was the only one incapable of breaking fifty. Still, no one had called him "fatso" or "spaz." Here was the first real, tangible evidence Danny had that being an heir could be a valuable thing.

He faced the pins, squared his feet and shoulders. Then he stepped bravely toward the line and let her go. Excellent form. Followed by a quick *clunkety-clunk-bumpety* and then the sound of the ball dropping off the lane into the gutter.

"Nice try, Big Dan!"

"We'll get 'em next time."

When it was all over the All Stars went to Shakeys together. Danny ordered several pizzas and pitchers of beer. When the beer came Ramon raised his glass in tribute to the newest team member.

"But, Ramon," Danny protested good-naturedly. "I smelled."

"Is okay," insisted Ramon. "You try."

The party broke up around ten. Danny made sure to grab the check. Bobby and Phil went home in Bobby's truck. Sheila, Sandy, and Tommy went home in Sandy's Toyota. Ramon and his wife and seven kids went home in Ramon's Chevy. Danny looked around and suddenly realized he and Doris were the only two people left in the parking lot.

"Oh, darn," she said. "I guess I need a ride home."

It was light out. Morning. Her bedroom had fuzzy blue wallpaper. It looked like the inside of someone's van. He heard something tapping lightly at the window.

"What's that noise?"

"It's the rain, babe."

"It can't be. It doesn't rain in L.A. in the summer."

"You're not in L.A. You're in Anaheim."

He heard a car splash through a puddle out on the
street. "Must be the smog. Gotta be." His eyes started
to close on their own. "What day is this?"

"Wednesday. I'm Doris."

He laughed and kissed her pulpy lips. "You I
remember."

Indeed. He'd never experienced such a night of wild
carnal pleasure. This was just the kind of thing that
he'd decided only happened to other, thinner people.
This Doris, she was nuts. And so, he discovered, was
he. He'd been holding in a lot since he came to work.
Frustration. Uncertainty. His Fear. With Doris, it all
burst out. Ferociously. He barely knew himself.

He liked it. He liked Doris. He liked Doris's tongue.

"Can I ask you a personal question?" he asked. "Why
me?"

She smiled. "You're cute."

Danny frowned. "I always thought cute was another word for, you know, not cute."

"Not to me. To me it's another word for . . . sexy."

He lay there beaming. *Sexy.*

A pot of coffee and a shower in his room at the Holiday Inn woke him up. True, one eye still kept wanting to close. True, when he tried to take a whiz much
of it ended up in the wastebasket over by the bedroom window. Still, he felt terrific.

Yes, there was a definite spring to his step as he made
his way down the Pier West corridor. He smiled and
waved good morning to people. And when he passed
Doris's desk, he was pleased to see how discreet she
was. Neat, somber dress. Correct, professional smile.
Nothing to indicate that she'd been squatting on his
face, naked, only an hour before. He wouldn't mind
seeing more of her. A lot more.

Abe was looking through some files outside the sales
department. "Morning, D.L.," he said. "Understand
you're some bowler."

"It was fun. Pop, did it used to rain in L.A. in the summer?"

"Never. It's the smog."

"That's what I thought."

"Want me to call Mayor Yorty about it?" Abe chuckled and headed down the hall toward his office.

Pip wasn't at her desk. Danny sat down at his and began to hunt through his briefcase for the article Irv had given him. Pip appeared in a minute with his coffee. She put it down on his desk. He said good morning. She didn't. He thanked her for the coffee. She didn't say you're welcome.

"Something wrong, Pip?"

"Wrong?" She was chewing on her lower lip, which was white.

"Look, I'm hoping we've developed to where we can communicate with each other. If there's anything I can do, even if it's just to listen . . ."

She glanced inquiringly at his office door.

"Go ahead," he assured her.

She closed it. Then she sat. Then she erupted. "Damn you! How could you *do* this to me?!"

"W-wha—?"

"I thought you were *smart!* Damn you!"

Danny reddened. "D-Doris?"

"D-Doris," she fired back, mimicking him.

"How did you—?"

"*Everyone* knows. Everyone *always* knows."

"So what?" Danny demanded forcefully. His head began to pound. "Does my father know?"

"The boss is the last to find out these things."

"Who tells him?"

"I do. You he'll be pissed at. Me he's going to fire."

"I think you're overreacting a little."

"The hell I am. I made a deal with him. I'm under explicit orders to protect you from this sort of thing. And report to him if I fail. I've been *so* careful. Damn,

I should have learned to bowl. How could you do this to me?!"

"I didn't know I was doing it to you. What kind of crazy deal is that, anyway?"

"The kind that gets you this kind of job."

Buzzzz . . .

She reached across, answered his phone. "Mr. Levine's office." She listened, then handed him the receiver. "For you," she said dryly.

Danny took it. "Hello?"

"It's me," said Doris. "I just wanted you to know I'd really like to be tied up and fucked up the ass."

"B-by me?"

"Who else, babe?"

Danny shifted in his chair and glanced up at Pip, who was glaring at him. "Sounds great. Can't talk now. Bye." He hung up quickly.

Pip was still glaring at him.

Danny sat back as far back as he dared.

"I'm really disappointed in you, Danny. But I'm not the one who matters. It's Irv and Larry who do. Now they'll think you're a lightweight."

Danny shrugged. "So what? I don't care what they think of me."

"You *have* to care. They're looking to you to be their leader."

"They are?"

"Of course."

Danny massaged his temples. "I'm not here to lead anybody anywhere. I'm strictly here for a year. And besides, I'm not exactly leadership material. I'm a very average person. Always have been."

"No! You're a born leader. You're genuine. Sensitive. Fair. People respond to you."

"They do?"

"*I* did. By the way, I'd start monitoring for discharges if I were you."

"Whew, you're tough."

"You don't know how tough I am."

"I don't think I want to find out."

"Tell Doris it's over. Tell her right now and I won't say anything to your father. Chances are he'll never find out. Dump her or I tell him and throw myself on his mercy. That's my offer, take it or leave it."

"Let's calm down, okay? Have six or seven Excedrin. Talk this out." He fished several Excedrins out of his top drawer and downed them with his coffee.

"Are you going to keep seeing her?" Pip demanded.

"I didn't *plan* to *start* seeing her. It just happened. I don't see why I can't enjoy myself like other people do, as long as I do my job well. I don't accept this whole situation. I'm not a little kid. Just because he happens to be my father . . . Besides, he isn't going to fire you."

"Oh, he will."

"He'd never do something like that. It's unreasonable. It's vindictive. It's—"

"It's his company."

"Pip, give me some credit, okay? I've known the man for twenty-three years."

"You know him as a father. You don't know him as a boss. People here are terrified of him. They call him . . ."

"Call him what?"

"The Czar."

"Pop?"

"Yes."

"Well, I'm sorry I didn't know about this arrangement you made. But I assure you you've got nothing to worry about. He told me himself you're the best secretary in the whole place."

"You're not going to dump Doris?"

"I am not."

She got to her feet. "Okay. Been nice working with you."

"Pip, is this absolutely necessary?"

"I made a deal." With that she headed straight down the hall toward Abe's office.

Danny sighed, found the article Irv had given him, and started reading it. He couldn't concentrate. Every time somebody walked by his door he kept wondering if it was Pip. The *Czar*?

When she returned, Pip was carrying an empty carton, which she placed on top of her desk. She opened the middle drawer and began to empty its contents into the box.

Danny went to her. "You're kidding, right?"

"Of course not," she said.

"But this is absurd!"

Secretaries began to look at the two of them.

"Lower your voice," ordered Pip in a sharp whisper.

"You're *not* getting fired," he whispered back. "Just . . . stop that emptying."

She ignored him. He sat her down in her desk chair. She bounced back up.

"*SIT!*" he commanded.

She sat.

He stormed down the corridor to Abe's office, swept past two salesmen waiting outside, opened the door, and slammed it behind him. Abe was on the phone. He smiled at Danny, motioned for him to sit down. Danny was too angry to sit. He paced. Abe's office was small and bare, save for the pictures of Danny that were all over the place—baby pictures, bar mitzvah pictures, school graduation pictures. A glass wall divided Abe's office from the warehouse floor. Abe's desk faced it. He liked to keep an eye on things. Danny paced the carpet, fuming.

Abe laughed into the phone. "Lou? You're a *gonif*, Lou. Gotta go. A big shot just walked in." Abe winked at Danny. "Good-bye, Lou." He hung up the phone. "What's up, D.L.?"

"How dare you fire Pip?" Danny demanded.

"She and I made a verbal contract," he replied calmly. "She violated it. She got *yentzed*. Simple."

"But she didn't do anything!"

"She didn't?"

"No!"

"Who did?"

"I did," Danny replied.

"Uh-huh."

"Ohhh . . . I get it. You're making an example of her. Teaching me a lesson, like I'm seven years old. Well, I'm *not* going to play these games, Pop! You've *got* to deal with me like I'm any other employee!"

"You're *not* any other employee!" Abe hollered. "For you, for a young man in your position, for every act there is a consequence! Where's your judgment, huh?! In your pants?! You're gonna be the boss some day!" Abe calmed himself. "I told you not to fool around with the girls here. You chose not to listen. You violated lesson number . . . what number was it?"

"I forget."

"Don't forget again. If there's one thing I can't stand it's a guy who walks around the office with his—"

"Dick in his hand."

"Get your goddamned love life in order. Now get back to work."

Danny sat. "Take Pip back."

"Pip's gone."

"She's bright and loyal and you can't fire her just to punish me. You can't treat another human being that way. Take her back."

Abe swiveled in his chair, looked out the window at the parking lot. "I can't. She'd take it as a sign of weakness. Never do another thing I told her."

"She'd take it as a sign of humanity."

Abe frowned. "What's that supposed to mean?"

"Did you know they call you The Czar?"

Abe smiled proudly. "Had to work hard to get that kind of respect."

"Pop, you don't have to be a monster to get good results from people."

"What the hell do you know about it?"

"Take her back or I'm quitting. I mean it. I'm out of here. Gone. You can sell my car." Danny got up, started for the door.

"Kiddo, kiddo. Wait. C'mon, let's not go to war over this."

Danny stopped. "Take her back?"

Abe sighed. "Strictly as a personal favor to you. But only, and I repeat, only, if you stop seeing Doris. Never again. I want your word."

Danny hesitated.

"If you lie to me, I'll know."

This was true. If there was one person Danny couldn't lie to it was Abe.

"All right," he said. "It's a deal."

"And if this ever happens again with another secretary . . ."

"What, you're going to fire me?"

"And I thought this was going to be fun," Abe said sourly.

"That's the difference between us, Pop. I knew it wasn't going to be."

Pip was waiting for him at her desk. He motioned for her to join him in his office.

"He reconsidered," he told her.

She widened her eyes.

Danny leaned against his desk. "Pip, I want you to know that this kind of thing, like what happened last night, it doesn't happen to me very often. Or very occasionally. Or ever. And it won't happen again."

"Good. And thank you. I like this job."

Danny sat. "I don't know what to say to her."

"Tell her you made a mistake."

Danny started thinking about Doris's tongue again. "I guess I'd better," he said reluctantly.

"No, you'd better not. I'll tell her. Otherwise there might be a scene. Bad personal p.r. for you."

"I can't ask you to do something like that."

"You didn't. I volunteered. Actually, I think I'll like it."

"No, I can't let you clean up my—"

"Comes with the—"

"I'll handle it," Danny assured her.

"I insist."

"Well, if it means that much to you."

"Thank you. May I fire her if she gets ugly?"

Danny mulled it over. "No. If she's no longer an employee I'll be tempted to call her. She might stay in touch with people here. It might get back to—"

"You are so naive."

"I am?"

"If she's not working here she's not *going* to see you. Didn't her motives occur to you?"

"I didn't much care what her motives were. At least, not last night." Danny scratched his head. North. He should have headed north. But he'd been north. "Wanna use my office?"

"No, thanks. This sort of thing ought to be done in the ladies' room. Just do me one favor."

"Get my love life in order?"

She nodded.

"I thought I had."

Doris paid a visit to the ladies' room not long after that. When she strode past, Pip waited one second, then got up from her desk and scurried after her.

Danny went back to trying to read Irv's article. After a minute he heard the ladies' room door being flung open. He held his breath. Doris charged past his office, cheeks reddened, nostrils flared, not looking at him. He let his breath out in relief. An instant later she returned and hurled her "Doris" coffee mug at him. He ducked just in time, as it smashed against his new bamboo shade. The "DO" went one way, the "IS" the other. Danny didn't find the "R."

He lunched at his desk, on a tuna boat and four Milky Way bars from the poison wagon that stopped in the parking lot three times a day. The rain had given way to steamy sun. Irv jogged by him while Danny was waiting in line. They exchanged waves. Irv wore a yellow nylon sweatsuit and his gas mask. He looked like he belonged on Pluto.

As soon as Pip went out to run some errands, Danny drove around La Mirada until he found a florist. There he bought a dozen roses. He left them on her desk. When she came back she arranged them in a Pier West vase and placed them next to her type-writer. Then she sat down and smiled.

Newt Biddle's house was still the only one on Kelton Avenue that had a lawn that was never wa-tered or mowed. The grass grew in great green and white clumps, spilling out onto the sidewalk, the curb, and the cement path to the front steps. It was a white one-story Spanish stucco house with a red tile roof. The paint was peeling. The window in the front bed-room, the one where Newt's kid sister Jenny slept, was still broken.

Newt's VW bus, Queenie, was parked in the drive-way.

A teenaged girl in cut-offs and a tie-dyed T-shirt sat on the front steps staring intently at an album cover. Possibly, Danny figured, she was pursuing indepen-dent studies at Catatonic State.

Danny sat across the street in his MG, tie loosened, top down, Twinkie stuffed in his mouth. He washed it down with some cold chocolate milk from the car-ton, bit into another one from the handy 12-pack in his lap, and thought about going in. Just to say hello. See what was happening.

An old faded red panel truck with a Clancy Muldoon

Plumbing and Heating sign on the side pulled up in front of Newt's. A grubby-looking freak in a flannel shirt and torn jeans climbed out and scuffled barefoot out back to the garage, where Newt usually hung out. Danny recognized him as someone he and Newt had once dealt acid to. Jesse was his name. Certainly that was a safe guess. Every other freak in West L.A. called himself Jesse, even if his given name was Nachum.

Jesse being here meant Newt was still dealing. And Danny knew what that meant, too: Newt was still dropping.

Danny put his Twinkies on the passenger seat and started up the MG. On acid Newt was intolerant, inflexible, and overbearing. Either you agreed with what he, in his humble opinion, believed or you were a turkey. Newt on acid was the person Danny had had to get away from—if he wanted to become a grownup.

Danny was just about to pull away from the curb when there was a flurry behind him and the passenger door flew open and someone hopped in next to him.

"Hello, Daniel," Newt said coolly.

Stunned, Danny nodded at him.

"Jesse said someone with rather short hair was parked outside in a green MG," Newt explained. "I assumed it was you, but I had to make certain. I have to be rather careful these days."

Danny nodded again.

"Aren't you going to say anything, Daniel?"

"You're sitting on my Twinkies."

Newt snorted, which was what he did instead of laughing. He reached under his khaki cutoffs and produced the flattened box. The white filling was now squishing out of them. Danny snatched the box from him and tossed it grumpily behind his seat.

Newt reached over and shut off Danny's ignition. Then he punched the cigarette lighter and removed a Marlboro from the pocket of his frayed, wrinkled,

blue oxford button-down. Newt's tangled blond hair,
parted on the side, fell to his shoulders. His cleft Biddle chin needed a shave. Somehow his finely-chiseled
face looked different. Danny couldn't place it at first.
Same patrician nose. Same even blue eyes. Same upturned, impertinent upper lip. Finally Danny realized
Newt was now wearing a small diamond in the lobe
of his left ear.

Newt lit his Marlboro and inhaled it deeply. Then
he sat back and put his feet—which were in desert
boots that Jenny had painted to look like wing-tip
shoes—up on the dashboard. He sighed contentedly.
He didn't seem to be stoned, though he never had. He
was so calm and reserved that he'd gone to classes at
Harding on acid and nobody had suspected until he
mentioned it.

"Been back long, Daniel?"

"A few weeks. I'm . . ." Danny hesitated. Why was
it still so important to him what Newt thought of
him? "I'm working for my pop."

"I see . . ."

I promised him a year."

Newt pursed his lips. "It's a profound step in the
wrong direction, in my humble opinion."

"Doing it is the only way to find out for sure,"
Danny countered.

"The present economic system is outmoded," Newt
declared. "For sure. It's institutionalized inequality.
It shall fall. I like your suit."

"Do you really?" asked Danny, pleased.

"Yes. Very tasteful."

"Thanks. What are you up to?"

Newt flicked his cigarette ash out onto the curb.
"We're raising money to buy a farm in Oregon. Possibly Washington. Anywhere we can find ourselves a
nice spread."

"Like the old Velveeta spread?" Danny grinned. An
old Mad magazine joke.

Newt didn't appreciate it. "Actually, this is quite serious, Daniel. We'll grow our own food. Each of us will be free to pursue our own ambitions. Jenny can paint. I'll be doing what I believe to be my life's work—the launching of a structured alternative society. A small community of like-minded souls living in cooperation instead of competition, peace instead of war. We'll have our own school. Our own council, each member a vote. Those who want to join us may do so, provided they are cool."

"And who decides that?"

"I do," Newt replied, Biddle jaw stuck out firmly.

"Uh-huh."

"We'll live the alternative—by example. It's what we were born to do. We alone have the vision, the absence of fear. We'll prove our way is right. Other farms will join us. Other communities. Cities. States. Capitalism will fall. Greed will end. A new day will dawn. That, Daniel, is what I will be doing."

Danny glanced over at him, waiting for the punch line. There wasn't one. Newt was perfectly serious. Danny cleared his throat. "You're going to save the world?" he asked uneasily.

"Somebody has to save it."

"You really believe it's going to be you?"

"I do."

"You shitting me?"

"I am not."

"No offense, but it might not be a bad idea to cut back on psychedelics for a while," Danny said carefully. "What you're talking about . . . it's an acid fantasy. It's all going on in your head. It *seems* real, but it isn't. It isn't *life*."

"Hmm. Yes, well, it's like I've always said, Daniel: Life sucks, but at least it's short."

"You ought to cut back," Danny repeated. "Seriously."

"I know what I'm doing, Daniel. Don't concern yourself, though I am touched."

"How are you raising the money for this farm?"

"Kilos, mostly. Quantities of them. The Goldstein brothers inherited our old lid traffic." Newt tossed his cigarette in the street, sat up. "Did you want to come inside, Daniel? Stimulating conversation is somewhat scarce these or any days."

Kilos. That was heavy trafficking. That was *dangerous.*

"That's okay," Danny said.

"Suit yourself." Newt climbed out of the MG.

"Want to get a burger some time or something?" Danny asked.

"Thank you, Daniel, but I really can't leave. Business, you know. And no one I can really count on— now that you've gone."

Danny nodded.

"What exactly did you want, Daniel?"

"Dunno."

"No offense, but you'd best not sit out here like this any longer. You're making the folks inside a tad paranoid." Newt gave him a half wave. "Until later." He crossed the street toward his house.

"Hey, Newt?" Danny called.

"Yes, Daniel?"

"Peeenis!"

Their ancient greeting.

Newt snorted. Then he promptly fell to the lawn and treated Danny to a world-class spaz attack. He totally let loose—limbs flailed, spittle flew, eyes rolled. It was a genuine blast from their past. Danny was tempted to join him. Hadn't chewed any grass in ages. But the stains would never come out of his suit.

Abruptly Newt stopped, jumped to his feet, and bowed from the waist.

Danny applauded.

The teenaged girl with the album cover never looked up.

Danny waved good-bye and pulled away, bothered by what had happened to his old partner in crime. How could somebody who was so smart, so full of ideas . . . Maybe Mouse had hit on it. Newt's whole blue-blood family was on a stairway going down. Had been since they fled Locust Valley in debt. Newt was running away from the truth as his mother had. He was just using a different drug.

A farm sounded wonderful. Sitting on the porch. Taking a dip in the watering hole. No hassles. No deals. Sounded great, except for the fact that you had to be ripped off of your gourd to believe in it. That was no answer. That was the way to madness, wasn't it?

Possibly he would not drop by Newt's again.

Danny was at Sunset and Hilgard by the time he realized why he even stopped there in the first place. Newt had always been the one person Danny told things to. Only Newt knew that Danny believed *2001: A Space Odyssey* was the most boring movie ever made. And agreed. Only Newt knew what Danny's Fear was. And understood.

Danny had actually gotten laid. He wanted to tell Newt about it.

"They're looking to you to be their leader. . . ."

Danny tossed and flopped and thrashed, unable to sleep. It was a little past 2 A.M. Warm in his room, but not that warm. Something else was keeping him up.

"You could help make Pier West the model of a modern, socially responsible corporation. . . ."

This wasn't what he wanted.

"Think about the five hundred and fifty people. . . ."

He didn't want to care. About the company. About its problems. About its people. This wasn't what he wanted.

"I don't want some jerk with a slide rule. I want you. . . ."

His heart was pounding now. His chest felt tight.

"They're looking to you to be their leader. . . ."

He threw the sheet aside, put on a pair of shorts, and waddled downstairs. There was food down there.

The patio screen door was open. The Czar was sitting outside in a deck chair, gazing down at the sleeping city, sipping from a steaming mug. Coco dozed at his feet.

They hadn't said much to each other at dinner. It was not, Danny now realized, a good idea to quarrel with your boss if you lived with him.

He scavenged through the refrigerator, came away with a brisket sandwich, pickles, and a bottle of cold beer. He went outside with it and sat in a chair next to Abe. Coco stirred but didn't yap at him. Progress.

"Trouble sleeping, kiddo?"

Danny nodded, munching. "Up like this often, Pop?"

"Often." Abe sipped from his mug. "Want me to fix ya a hot water and milk? Settles the stomach."

Danny crammed more sandwich in his mouth. "No, thanks."

"What are ya drinking, beer?"

"Something wrong with that?"

Abe shot him a look. "Drink whatever you want. What do I care?"

Danny took a gulp from the bottle. "What happened today . . . I'm sorry if I let you down, but you've set awfully high standards for me."

"Those are the only kind of standards there are. And you didn't let me down. You made a mistake. Nothing wrong with making a mistake, as long as you learn from it."

"Gee, I sure wish you'd stop doing that."

"Doing what?"

"Lecturing me like I'm a kid. I'm not."

Abe sighed. "I realize that. The thing is, you've been a kid for as long as I've ever known you. You've always been a kid. Gimme time. I'll get used to it."

Abe rubbed his neck, groaned softly. "Been meaning to tell ya—I like the way you handled that business with Natey."

"Thanks."

"Getting anywhere with your report?"

"I think so."

"Good. Knew you'd make headway."

Danny gobbled down the last of his sandwich. "I'm not so sure you're going to be too crazy about my findings."

"That's just what I want. A fresh, critical look. No punches pulled."

"You sure?"

"Positive."

Danny felt himself relaxing a little. Sure, Abe had asked for this, hadn't he? Besides, the company was *his* problem. Danny would move on. Camp out in the desert for a while. Clean out. But then what?

"*Tsuris*, kiddo?"

Danny shrugged.

"It's the job, isn't it?"

"What makes you say that?"

"It's three o'clock in the morning, you got *tsuris* and you don't wanna talk about it. What else could it be?"

Danny drained his beer. "Chip off the old block, huh?" he commented ruefully.

Abe winked at him. "How ya like the stores?"

"They're okay. Most of the merchandise seems to be Oriental or Danish."

"That's what people want."

"I don't."

Abe leaned forward in his chair a little. "You don't?"

"Uh-uh. That got me to thinking there might be a new market for old stuff, from the thirties. Reproductions."

Abe scratched his chin. "You mean like Fiestaware, right? Not a bad idea, kiddo. Only, that art deco doesn't last. I was around for it. It's nice, but people didn't want to live with it after a while. Too weird."

Danny shrugged. "Okay. Just thought I'd mention it. Guess I'll head back up to—"

"Where ya going? I didn't say no, did I? We could do some of it. But we gotta incorporate it into a bigger line. Something broader. Something with . . . Wait a minute. Wait just one minute . . ." Abe got to his feet and began to pace around on the pavement in his sleepers, warming to a thought. "Yeah . . . yeah . . . yeah!"

"Yeah what?"

"What are those lamps called, those Victorian lamps?"

"Tiffany lamps?"

"*Tiffany* lamps. And there's all that other Victorian stuff, right? The bathroom decor. The mirrors. The hat stands. All knockoffs, like you said. Then you got your *early* American. Your quilts. Your lace tablecloths. Your . . . what else is early American?"

"Indians?"

"C'mon, be serious."

"Hooked rugs?"

"Hooked rugs! What else? C'mon!"

"Pottery?"

"Pottery!"

"Baskets?"

"Baskets! Ya see it, kiddo? *Pier West comes home.* We'll call it . . . we'll call it *American Heritage.* Feature all the different eras. We got that big bicentennial thing coming up in four years. We can tie in with that— people'll be patriotic as hell. We'll get the Koreans going on it right now. Beat the pants off Import Barn. Kiddo, this is big!"

Abe seemed genuinely excited. Nothing Danny had ever said or done in his entire life had gotten quite this reaction out of him.

"You really think so, Pop?" he said, pleased.

"I sure as hell do! Good thinking, Maynard. Good thinking!"

"Here's another thought," Danny said. "Why buy it from the Koreans? Why not manufacture it ourselves? That way we can control the cost and the quality."

"That's asking for trouble."

"But doesn't it make sense?"

"There's an old, old saying in business, kiddo: Don't fix something that ain't broken." Abe gulped from his mug. "*American Heritage.* I like the way that sounds! My boy, I'm very proud of you! I always knew you had it in you. You and me. This is what I've dreamed of. I'll go get us a pad. We'll make some notes. You stay right there. Stay there and think!"

Chapter Eight

The Century Plaza Hotel sat in the middle of a planned complex of high-rise office buildings, apartment towers, and shopping plazas that had all been the back lot of 20th Century Fox Studios when Danny was a teenager. Century City made Danny uneasy. He didn't feel old enough to be older than an entire city.

He was meeting Mouse here for an after-work drink. Pip had scheduled the date at Mouse's request. Danny had been out of the office most of the day, visiting stores in Monrovia and Montebello. Mouse told her Danny was to be here at 6:30 and remember one thing and one thing only: act natural.

As opposed to what, Danny wondered.

The lobby was large and airy. There was a sunken lounge where elegantly dressed business people sipped cocktails. A pianist played show tunes. Little kids in bathing suits ran by dripping wet on their way from the pool. Danny looked around. An absolutely stunning blonde sat in intimate conversation with a small, dark-haired young guy. The guy jumped to his feet and waved to Danny. Mouse Stern.

Act natural.

"Dan Levine. I'd like you to meet Mandy West."

She was even more gorgeous from close up, though not in an inviting sort of way. Her cascading hair was sprayed hard into place. Her eyes and cheeks and lips were so heavily made up she looked like she'd been dipped in lacquer. She wore a white silk blouse unbuttoned to her waist and no bra. Her breasts were seriously pendulous. Danny couldn't help but notice this. When she held her hand out for him to shake it, she held it so that his eyes fell right *there*. Her hand was cool and manicured; her peach nails matched her lipstick.

"Pleased to meet you, Mr. Levine," she said in a soft, little girl's voice.

"Likewise," he said. "And it's Danny."

She smiled at him. Her eyes were like a doll's— innocent, wide open, unblinking.

He smiled back. Began to play with his tie. Caught himself. Sat. Shot a look at Mouse to find out what exactly was happening.

Mouse was looking for a waiter. When the waiter came over, Mandy ordered a ginger ale. Danny ordered a beer. Mouse ordered a kir. Then he cleared his throat and plowed right in.

"A lot of people like to know what an agent does," he said. "I like to define it as someone who brings together people who'll feel comfortable with each other. People who have interests in common. People like you two. Dan, for instance, grew up right here in L.A."

"Did you?" she exclaimed.

"Mandy's from Downey," Mouse said. "And she's very into skydiving."

"I enjoy taking physical risks," she said.

"Good," said Danny. "That makes one of us."

His beer came. He gulped half of it down quickly.

"Tell him about your experiences, cookie," Mouse said, taking Mandy's hand. "Don't be bashful. You're among friends."

"Well, I've made several appearances in high school theatrical productions," she said in a practiced, careful way.

"Major productions," Mouse pointed out.

"I appeared in the Downey Summer Theater production of *A Streetcar Named Desire.*"

"She was Blanche."

"As well as *Othello.*"

"She was Desdemona."

"For the past six months I've been studying acting with Joan Darling, in addition, of course, to making promotional appearances associated with my modeling career."

"Tell him about your modeling."

Mandy blushed and looked down at her hands, which were folded in her lap. "I was Miss April, 1970, in *Playboy* magazine."

"Under the name of Kerri Lang," said Mouse.

"It has been a very fascinating experience for me," she pointed out. "I've met a number of very fascinating people, thanks to Hef."

"She used to go with Wilt Chamberlain."

"And now," Mandy went on, "I'm hoping to branch out into the field of motion picture performing."

"A lot of 'em are doing it," Mouse advised.

Bee-beep . . . bee-beep . . . bee-beep . . .

It was the alarm on Danny's new watch. Somehow he'd accidentally set it to go off every day at this hour and had yet to figure out how to unset it.

Bee-beep . . . bee-beep . . . bee-beep . . .

He grinned sheepishly and pushed the button that stopped the beeping. Then he reached for his beer.

"What kind of picture is it you're producing, Danny?" Mandy asked.

She caught him mid-gulp. He sprayed it—air-mailed suds all over the peanuts and the ashtray and her.

"My what—?"

"Your movie," Mouse said quickly to him from between his teeth. "I didn't want to give away too much."

"It's . . . it's . . ."

"Wouldn't you call it a sci-fi, Dan?" suggested Mouse.

He felt a swift kick in his right shin. "Okay," he agreed slowly.

She nodded, sincerely interested. "Those are my favorite kind."

Mouse put an arm around her. "Cookie, why don't you go clean up." He indicated the bathroom with a nod of his head.

"Okay. Excuse me, please, Danny."

She got to her feet and started for the bathroom. She wore tight jeans and high-heeled boots. Every head in the place turned as she passed.

"What are you doing?" Danny demanded when she was out of earshot.

"Trying to bang the most beautiful woman I've ever had a legit shot at. You, however, are blowing it, you big fat goon."

"I'm pretending to be a movie producer so you can get laid?"

"Relax. She has friends. And girls like that don't hang around with pigs, believe me."

"I believe you, Stern. I believe you. Only, I'm not gonna do it. I don't believe in deceiving a woman in order to get her in bed. It happens to be my personal philosophy."

"Do well by it?"

"It kind of goes in waves. And that's not the point."

"What is?"

"Wendy. You happen to be married to her, remember?"

"Levine, I don't believe in deception, either. That's what's behind this whole open marriage thing Wendy and I have. That's the very reason I insisted on it."

"So you can fuck around any time you want."

"Wendy can, too. It's out in the open. No hypocrisy. That's what I hate."

"So you'll tell Wendy all about this?"

"You crazy? She'd beat the crap outta me."

"But I thought—"

"We agreed we'd each do what we wanted. We didn't agree we'd *talk* about it. That's tacky."

"Look, you want to fuck around on her, that's your business, okay? But I'm not going to help you. I'm her friend, too, and I don't think it's fair to her. It isn't fair to this Mandy either, deceiving her just so you can ball her."

"What kinda sleaze do you think I am? This is no quick wham on the couch. I'm smitten. Have been ever since she came into the office. I can't get this girl outta my mind. But no way she'll give me the time of day unless she thinks I can do her career some good. She's gotta think that."

"So why don't you introduce her to a *real* Hollywood producer. Isn't that what your job is?"

"I can't. Annie turned her down cold as a client. The girl can't act, and Playmates are a dime a dozen in this town. Twelve a year, every year. So I'm kind of handling her on the side on Annie's behalf, only Annie doesn't know about it, see?"

Danny shook his head. "Has it occurred to you that you could get fired for doing something like this?"

"By Annie? Never. She'd admire my enterprise. Besides, for that girl it'd be worth getting fired. It's why I'm in the business. What do you say, Levine?"

"Won't Mandy notice something's kind of funny when I don't hire her for my 'movie'?"

"I'll tell her your deal fell apart. Happens all the time."

"Then what?"

"I'll comfort her."

"Have it all figured out, huh?"

Mouse grinned. "Uh-huh."

"This is the stupidest thing you've ever done. Trust me."

"Will you do it?"

"Absolutely not."

"I'd do it for you."

"We're not a hundred percent alike."

"C'mon, Levine. This is what pals do."

"No."

"Did I remember to say please?"

"No!"

"Did I remember to say you owe me?"

Danny frowned. "Owe you?"

"You lied to me. You told me you never banged Wendy. I know you did. She told me."

Danny reddened. "I did that to spare your feelings. Maybe I was wrong to, but—"

"Exact same thing I'm doing here. Sparing Wendy from telling her something that would only make her feel bad. Sparing Mandy from the sharks. This girl has no chance out there. She's sweet. Trusting. And she's getting fucked over by terrible guys. I'm the sweetest guy she'll ever meet—let alone get eaten out by for sixteen continuous hours." He groaned. "Oh God, here she comes." Mouse leaned toward Danny, lowered his voice. "I trusted you, Levine. You were the only one I really trusted. And you nailed me for it. You banged the woman I married and you lied to me about it. You hurt me deeply. Do this one little thing for me. That's not so much to ask, is it?"

Danny sat back and puffed out his cheeks, defeated. "I don't know why I ever bother to lie to people. I always get caught."

"How about another piña colada?"

A bit of her first one still remained on Rachel's downy upper lip. She dabbed at it with her cocktail napkin. "Actually, I'm kind of nauseous."

"Want me to take you home?"

"This feels like a date."

"It's not a date."

They were sitting in the bar of Chuck's Steak House in Marina Del Rey. It was Saturday night, and a lot of very loud, very forced assholes of both sexes were crammed in there with them—drinking and laughing and, occasionally, whooping. The guys wore Sundance Kid mustaches, hiphugger jeans, body shirts, and gold chains. The women wore long, shimmering dresses and heavy, clunky heels that looked hard to walk on. Rachel had on a peasant blouse and suede skirt and was so tense her stomach could have served handsomely as a Hank Aaron pitchback. Danny was sorry he had made the reservation.

He hadn't known Chuck's had become a singles hangout. He remembered it as a quiet place with a nice view of the boats, a man-sized surf and turf combo, and a great salad bar where you could take as much of any kind of salad you wanted and keep coming back for more. When he was sixteen he thought that was neat. Actually, he still thought that was neat. What wasn't neat was all of these people, and the Stevie Wonder thumping away on the jukebox, and the Aramis and cigarette smoke and desperation in the air.

"It's not a date," he repeated. "It's a thank you."

"For what?"

"Your suggestion about the flowers. And your new approach. You were really on to something. It's made things a lot more palatable. Also confusing."

She shrugged noncommittally.

"Look, Rachel, you know me well enough to know I'm not gonna stick my tongue down your throat."

"That's true," she admitted.

Gee, she didn't have to agree *quite* so readily.

"I just wanted to see you, as a friend," Danny went on. "During the week is hard, because I get home late. I thought we could have dinner, talk. I need to talk to somebody. You seem to be the only person in the whole world who understands what I'm going through. Okay?"

She uncoiled a little. "Okay. But only if you do me one favor."

"Name it."

"Take me away from this place."

He took her to Malibu with the MG's top down and the wind blowing in her hair. He took her to their old beach and parked there alongside the vans and panel trucks.

The surfers were way out on their boards, bobbing like ducks while they held out for the big one. The setting sun made their wet skin shimmer like gold. Slim brown girls waited on the sand for them, their arms wrapped around their knees.

"Nothing changes down here, does it?" Danny said.

"Not a thing."

"It could be ten years ago."

"No, it couldn't."

She got out, kicked off her sandals, and started walking. Danny removed his shoes and socks and started after her, then stopped when he realized he was kicking sand into his cuffs. He rolled them up and caught up with her, stepping carefully to avoid the rocks, the sharp, broken shells, and the dead jellyfish which lay on the wet sand like big blobs of snot.

"So work isn't okay?" she asked.

"There are certain sacrifices. Personal, mostly. But I do have a chance to do something positive. Create new jobs, offer people lives of quality, like you said. That's what I'm concentrating on right now. My pop, he's a great businessman, only he doesn't think about the people much."

"That's your role."

"I have kind of a problem with that."

He used to dream about this—he and Rachel walking on this beach at sunset. Just the two of them. And now it was really happening, only they were talking about the office.

"Would this have to do with your greatest fear in life?" she asked.

"Yes, it would."

"I think I know what it is. You're afraid you'll sell out."

"Good guess. Only, wrong. I don't think we'll sell out as long as we believe in something. Stand for something."

"There is no we."

"You sound like your brother."

"You sound like you still think you're part of some group. There's no group. Just you."

Danny stepped down on something incredibly sharp, bit his lip, and kept going, trying not to limp. A pant leg unrolled, and his cuff filled with water.

"He and Wendy," Danny said. "What they have isn't my idea of a relationship."

"It's not a relationship at all."

"They think it is."

"They think it's *modern*. In art, as in life in general, modern is just another word for nonexistent. Deep down, they're very conventional people. They were both in a big hurry to be married. Mostly, I think they hated living alone. A lot of people do."

"I'm thinking about getting my own place."

"You'll like it."

Danny beamed. Clearly, she saw him as self-sufficient. Deep. "I guess I don't see how they can grow together as people in a relationship like they have."

"They won't. They'll grow apart. Have kids to hold themselves together. That won't work, so they'll get a divorce. The kids will get big. Spit in their faces. Never speak to them again. That's what happens when people get married."

"I don't think I want to get married."

"I never will."

"Would you and Rick . . . ?"

"If he hadn't died? Probably. I'm kind of conventional, myself."

She went over to a driftwood log and sat. Danny joined her. They sat in silence for a while, watching the sunset. It was very peaceful.

Bee-beep . . . bee-beep . . . bee-beep . . .

Danny sighed and pushed the button to stop his infernal watch alarm. Only this time it failed.

Bee-beep . . . bee-beep . . . bee-beep . . .

He tried another button. And another button.

Bee-beep . . . bee-beep . . . bee-beep . . .

"Here, let me," Rachel offered.

He handed over the watch. She placed it on the log between them and smashed it repeatedly with a large rock until it was silent.

Danny grinned. "Now why didn't I think of that?"

"I have a confession to make," she said. "You asked me at the wedding if I blamed myself for Ricky's death. I said I didn't."

"And you do?"

"No, that's not it. To tell you the truth, Ricky's death . . . it sounds so terrible to say this out loud . . . Ricky's death was actually the best thing that's ever happened to me. I was so *relieved* when he died. See, I wanted to break up with him. For *years*. Only, I couldn't. This way, it was like my prayers were answered. I'm thrilled when I wake up in the morning and realize he's dead. Every day. And then I'm consumed by guilt for feeling that way. Every day." She looked at him. "Still want to be my friend?"

"Why didn't you just end it?"

"I'm weak. I'm gutless. I'm a total coward."

"Gee, you ought to be a little harsher on yourself."

"It's true, damn it. And now I've been given a second chance, a chance to really be *me*, only I don't know who the hell I am. Pretty silly, huh?" She wrung her hands. "I've always envied you."

"Me?" asked Danny, surprised.

"You know who you are."

"Oh. Well, that's not so hard."

"No?"

"Uh-uh. What's hard is changing. Look, I . . . I know a thing like what happened with Rick isn't easy to shake off. But you shouldn't get so down on yourself. You've got a real lot going for you. You're just a little off the track right now, that's all. You'll get back on. I'm sure of it."

She glanced over at him. "How'd you get to be so sweet?"

"It has something to do with being fat."

"Would you tell me your greatest fear in life?"

"You first."

"Uh-uh." She scampered nimbly to her feet. "But I will show you my pots. Still want to see them?"

A lot of streets in Venice had given way to new townhouse-style condos that had subterranean garages with electronic gates. Rachel's street wasn't one of them. She lived off a canal on a dead end where dogs and kids ran loose. Her shack was set behind two large olive trees. A Mateus bottle filled with sand sat next to the blistering front door.

"That's for breaking the kitchen window with when I lock myself out," she explained as she unlocked the door and flicked on the lights. "I've had to three times so far."

"Why don't you keep a spare key out here instead?"

"Haven't got one."

Danny frowned. "So why don't you—?"

"Come on in."

Rachel's place wasn't so much messy as awry. Things like shoes that should have been on the floor were on top of tables. Things like mail and sunglasses that should have been on top of tables were on the floor. Still, it was very nice. In fact, Danny was pleased to note, she had the same taste he had. A fat old overstuffed sofa and easy chair sat before the fireplace in the living room. The big kitchen was equipped with Depression-era appliances. There were two small bedrooms. One had a four-poster bed and a mirrored dresser in it. The other was bare except for an exercise mat and incense burner.

"I like your stuff," he exclaimed. "Where'd you get it?"

"Junk shops, flea markets. Most of it's not old enough to be called antiques."

She had a vegetable patch behind the house. There were neat, careful rows of lettuce, cucumber, squash . . .

Danny swallowed. "What's that lump there in the garden?" he asked uneasily. "The one that has a tail."

"It's a mouse," she said. "It's okay—it's dead."

"W-why don't you get rid of it?"

"It's mulching."

"Mulching?"

"Any kind of decomposed matter is good for the soil."

Danny shuddered and averted his eyes as they passed the garden, trying to be casual about it.

Her studio was in the garage, which backed onto an alley. There was a wheel, a kiln, big bags of clay. Brick-and-board shelves strained under the weight of her work—bowls, mugs, pitchers, vases, plates.

Danny found himself groping for just the right word to describe Rachel's pottery. Her style wasn't so much primitive as it was crude. Inexpert. Clumsy.

Crap—that was the word.

He nodded and smiled at her and kept his mouth shut. She flushed slightly.

She put on a record when they went back inside—*Nashville Skyline* by Bob Dylan. Then she put out the bread and cheese and wine Danny insisted they buy on the way. He didn't think she should skip dinner—she was already so thin. He wasn't crazy about skipping it himself. He sat in the big easy chair. She took the floor. He noticed she had shaved her legs. He wondered if their non-date had anything to do with it. He unscrewed the wine and poured them some.

She handed him some bread and cheese and searched his face. "So?"

He bit into it and chewed thoughtfully. "Actually, I don't know very much about art," he said.

"You know me."

"I do?"

"You have to tell me the truth, Danny. You're the only person I know who will. Do you like them? Tell me. Please."

"No, I don't. They look like the stuff you did when we went to Camp Hess Kramer."

She stared at him a second with her mouth slightly open. Then she said, "You're right. I have no talent. I know it."

"Wait, I didn't exactly say that."

"The problem with visual art is most people don't know the difference. *You* know."

"It's just an opinion. I could be wrong. I mean, I've never done anything artistic in my whole life."

"You used to play the violin."

"I repeat, I've never done anything artistic in my whole life." He drank some wine. "I'm sorry."

"No, don't be. I was going to drop out anyway."

"Don't do *that*. You should stay with it, if you enjoy it. What I think is . . ." He trailed off. He was starting to lecture her like some know-it-all junior professor.

"Go ahead, Danny."

"I think you shouldn't build your life around something if you don't really like it."

She smiled. "I thought you were the guy who didn't have any answers."

"That's when I'm with a girl."

"What am I, a fish?"

"You're a friend."

She *was*. Suddenly, it hit Danny—how much he'd grown up. Here he was, alone in a house with *Rachel Stern*, and he was doing fine. He wasn't worried their fingers might accidentally touch when she passed him the bread and that he'd drop it and get crumbs on her rug. He wasn't sweating. He wasn't sneaking looks at her perfect, pink bare toes. Well, he wasn't sweating.

"I will if you will," she said abruptly.

He coughed. "You will what?"

"Tell you my greatest fear."

"Hmm."

"Does anyone know yours?"

"Just Newt. You?"

"No one."

"Did Rick?"

"Don't make me laugh."

He poured them some more wine. "Okay. Sure. What the hell. My greatest fear in life . . ."

"Yes . . . ?"

"My greatest fear . . . is that I'm going to live a life that's already been lived by somebody else. There. Now you know it."

"Like who?"

"Like anybody, though I suppose my pop is a good place to start. It's been real hard for me to settle down, stay at anything for long. I get to thinking 'Big deal, this has already been done.' Or 'So what? Anybody can do this.' And then I bolt. It's sort of like having claustrophobia, except instead of being afraid of dark closets, I'm afraid of . . ."

"Life."

"I only get one shot. What if I blow it? What if I don't do the one thing nobody else will ever do if I don't do it?"

"Such as?"

"If I knew I wouldn't have a problem. This job I have now . . . I can already feel it *pulling* me in. I'm afraid I'll open my mouth one of these days and hear my pop's voice coming out. And then *me* will be lost. Forever." He took a sip of his wine. Well, at least she

hadn't laughed at him, told him he had a real stupid
fear. "What's yours?"

She shook her head. "Not yet."

"Why not?"

"You still have to sing the 'Mister Ed' theme song
for me."

"I don't know you well enough."

"What would you like to know about me?"

"Your greatest fear in life."

She looked into her glass. "That I'm not perfect."

"Who is?"

"I am. I mean, I'm supposed to be. I know it sounds
insane now, but guys used to put me up on this pedestal. Ricky . . . Ricky never really knew me. He just
thought I was this perfect girlfriend. Pretty. Smart.
Nice. Perfect. That's what they used to call me behind my back—Little Miss Perfect."

"They used to call me Blubstein. You have to get
past that stuff."

"I'm not. I think I *am* supposed to be perfect. Even
though what I really am good at is covering up my
flaws. It may be the only thing I am good at. And
lately, I've been losing my talent for that." She
laughed to herself sadly. "Little Miss Perfect is a mess."

"Everybody is a mess."

"I'm not supposed to be," she repeated.

Danny nodded. "I think you're a lot like me. I mean,
deep down, your fear is very similar to mine. You're
a hothouse plant, just like I am. I've been giving this
a lot of thought lately. You and me, we grew up in
a very strange, very special time and place. We've never
had to worry about any of the basics. Not like our
parents or our grandparents. We don't have to worry
about getting enough food on the table. Or about
being a Jew—we've never been kept out of a school
or a neighborhood. We've been coddled, protected.
Whatever we wanted, we got. And everybody else sort
of followed us. We didn't like Tony Bennett, so we

found the Beatles. Now our parents listen to them, and
wear blue jeans and love beads. We didn't believe in
Vietnam—bam, it's cool to oppose war. You think my
pop wanted to get his ass shot off in some trench in
France? No way. He just didn't have the luxury of asking if it was right or not. We're different. We're un-
believably spoiled, is what we are. And now . . . right
now, it's screwing us up. Because we're totally un-
equipped to handle any kind of disappointment or fail-
ure or day-in, day-out misery like other people are.
Things like, say, *work*. We expect to be happy. Nobody else does. They expect to suffer. We don't know
what it means to suffer. We're not tough. We're hothouse plants. And now . . . now it's cold outside."

Rachel yawned.

"Sorry. Didn't mean to go on."

"You didn't. How'd you get so smart?"

"Drugs and rock music, mostly. And I had you as
a friend. It's late. I'd better be going."

"You're not going anywhere, buster."

"I'm not?"

"It'll never work, kiddo," Abe told him from the
front steps.

"I don't see why not," said Danny from the driveway as he folded a garment bag into the passenger
seat of the MG. His duffel was already crammed in
the trunk.

"Shacking up never solves anything," said Ev.

"We're not 'shacking up,' Mom. This is strictly
platonic."

"What does that mean, sweetheart?"

"It means he wants to but Ruthie doesn't," Abe replied, sneaking a look under the MG to see if it was
dripping oil on his driveway.

"Rachel. And neither of us does," Danny assured
them.

"Then why are you moving in with her?" asked Abe.

Because she was reaching out to him. She needed him.

"Because," Danny said, "she has an extra room. We're good friends. It's cheap. Makes perfect sense."

"I don't know, kiddo. It sounds kooky to me."

"Kooky?"

"Will she cook for you?" Ev asked.

"I can cook for myself."

"Will she do your clothes?" Ev asked.

"I can wash them myself."

"So you'll be bringing them up here, sweetheart?"

"I'll be bringing them up here," he declared firmly.

"Let me ask you something, kiddo. Is this your idea of acting like an adult?"

"I never claimed to be an adult. All I said was I'm not a child." He slammed the trunk shut. "Look, I think it's best if I have my own place. You understand, don't you?"

"He wants his own place, Ev."

"If he wants his own place why is he shacking up with her?"

Danny sighed, exasperated. Abe and Ev weren't like those parents at Mouse and Wendy's wedding. They were becoming genuine old Jews. Still, he had to admit it was a bit comforting. This was how it was supposed to be.

He kissed Ev good-bye.

"See you Monday, Pop."

"See you Monday, D.L. . . . Hey, kiddo? Monday's the first."

Danny's report was due. "You'll get it," he promised. Boy would he get it.

"Say hello to Ruthie, kiddo. Kiddo? It'll never work."

"There's no such thing as a platonic relationship between two people when one of 'em has a dick and the other one doesn't."

Mouse and Wendy had come over the hill in matching sweatsuits to check out the houses for sale on the West Side. Danny had hung up his clothes and made up his bed. Well, mat, actually. But it was plenty comfy, the exercise mat. Firm. Now he and Mouse sat on the back steps. The two women were in the house.

"I don't see why it can't work," Danny said.

"Explain this to me—why would you want to live with someone, especially someone who, God bless her, isn't entirely screwed on straight, if you're not fucking her?"

Danny shrugged. There were some things you couldn't explain to Mouse. Things that had to do with honest human emotion, for instance. "I like it here," he replied.

"What's to like? It's a dump and a half. And you're sleeping on the floor, in case you didn't notice. Levine, you said you don't believe in deceiving anyone to get laid. Does that include yourself?"

"It'll be fine."

"Wait'll you bring a chick home for the night. She'll freak. I know her."

"Uh-uh. She brought that up herself. She said it was fine as long as we don't wake her up. And she can bring home a guy, too. It won't bother me."

Mouse shook his head, disgusted. "In matters of the heart, boychick, you're showing serious signs of being a born loser."

"You're just realizing that?"

Mouse stiffened. "Hey, what's that out there in the garden? That . . . lump?"

"It's a mouse."

"*Christ!*"

"It's dead."

"Shouldn't you—?"

"She wants to leave it there."

"Bullshit. She just doesn't want to go near it."

"She said it's good for the soil."

"And it was total bullshit. You're the man of the house now, Levine. It's *your* job."

Danny cleared his throat. "Think so?"

"Go take care of it."

"Maybe later."

"Jewish guy, huh?"

"You want to do it?"

"Hell no. I don't live here. Besides," Mouse added, peering at it, "he bears an uncanny resemblance to my Uncle Saul. That's old Highpockets Stern out there, and he's smiling right at me."

"Maybe I'll kind of kick some leaves over it."

"Go ahead."

"Nah, I'll still know it's there and that I didn't take care of it. Is there anyone you can hire?"

Rachel and Wendy came outside. Danny quickly changed the subject.

"You hungry?" he asked Rachel.

"He keeps trying to feed me," Rachel told Wendy. "No, Danny, I'm not hungry."

"You ought to have lunch," he said, nudging Mouse.

"Actually," Mouse said. "I'm kind of hungry."

"It's a conspiracy," said Rachel.

"C'mon," Danny said to Mouse. "Help me rustle something up."

"Who am I, the Galloping Gourmet?"

"Don't be such a sexist, Mickey," said Wendy. "You're embarrassing me."

"I am?"

"Yes, you are."

"Oh." Mouse seemed genuinely sorry. "Okay, cookie." He followed Danny inside.

"Gee, Stern. I hardly know you."

"What can I tell you, Levine. She's changed my whole life."

"Glad to hear it."

"Yeah, Mandy . . . she's special."

"Oh."

"She's amazing. She's better than I could possibly have imagined. Like dipping into a cream puff. Like

. . . Aw, the hell with this cock talk. This is *us* talking. I've never felt this way about a woman before. I'm intoxicated. I . . . I may even be in love. I'm not sure. What's love like?"

"Dieting."

There wasn't much in the refrigerator besides giant containers of plain yogurt and bags of lentils and oddly shaped squashes. He found some apples and the cheese they'd had for dinner the night before and unwrapped the bread.

"So what are you going to do?" he asked Mouse.

"I'm considering starring her in my first picture."

"This *is* serious."

"It's gonna be a campus protest comedy, I think. How's that sound?"

"Relevant."

Danny opened one drawer after another in pursuit of a bread knife. No luck.

"Good vehicle for Mandy," Mouse added. "She's got a real flair for comedy. As soon as I get a few thoughts down on paper, I'll start raising the money. I know I've been saying that for—"

"Days."

"But now I got what every man needs—a little motivation. I'm taking her to Vegas for the weekend."

"HEY, ROOMS?" Danny called out back. "WHERE ARE THE KNIVES?"

"IN THE TOASTER!" she replied.

"IS THAT BECAUSE YOU USUALLY NEED ONE WHEN YOU MAKE TOAST?"

"THAT'S RIGHT!"

"GOOD THINKING!"

Danny took one of the knives sticking out of the toaster. "Sure do find out things about people when you live with them," he observed, amused by the cute way her mind worked.

Mouse stared at him, mouth agape.

"Something wrong, Stern?"

"I take back everything I said before. Maybe this *will* work. You're as crazy as she is."

Danny started slicing the bread. "Vegas, huh? What about Wendy?"

"I told her I'm going to see a client's new act. Feel so guilty about it I got a rash all over my stomach." He rubbed his belly, then glanced down at it. "Sure hope it's gone by Friday."

They ate at the rickety wooden picnic table out in the yard. Afterward, Mouse actually helped Rachel clear it off. Danny stayed outside to keep Wendy company.

"I'm so happy the two of you got together," Wendy said. "Even if it is just platonic. It's nice. You can watch out for each other. Be here for each other."

"Right. That's the idea," agreed Danny, pleased that Wendy understood and surprised she was the one person who did.

"She already seems a hundred percent less gloomy to me. *We* should get together, you and me."

"Now, Wendy . . ."

"To talk," she added quickly. "No coming on. Just friends. Can't we have a platonic relationship, too?"

"Sure. Sure we can, Little Gal."

"How about next Saturday night? Michael has to go to Las Vegas to see a client."

Danny found himself examining the table.

"I'll make us dinner," she offered. "I just hate to be alone in that house."

"Sure. That'll be great."

After Mouse and Wendy left, Danny went inside to polish up his report. Rachel went out to work in her studio. Danny was just getting settled on his new bed, his papers spread in neat piles around him, when he heard a loud crash come from the studio. Followed by another. He jumped to his feet, hitched up his jeans, and waddled out there double-time.

Rachel was very calmly hurling every piece of her

pottery against the wall. She pitched her last remaining plate, shattering it, and started in on her mugs. And said, "Know what the L.A. City School District does with brain-damaged students? They make them go to special classes in the summer. Only the schools aren't air conditioned. So when the kids get too overheated the teachers take them outside and hose them down like hogs. It's absolutely criminal! Those kids deserve—"

"What sort of—"

"Special Ed. It's a two-year program." She looked around. Only her vases remained. She started in on those. "Michael thinks I should go to business school. He thinks anyone bright who doesn't apply themselves to making money is wasted."

"Yeah, I'm seriously considering putting him up for the Nobel Peace Prize next year."

She smiled in spite of herself. Her eyes scanned the empty shelves. "Well, so much for art," she concluded, starting for the door.

"Wait, where are you going?" asked Danny.

She frowned. "Inside."

"I can tell you never took shop."

"Shop?"

"Rule number two of the shop—you never start another job until you've finished cleaning up after your last one."

"What's rule number one?"

"No horseplay on the shop floor. Gee, I thought everybody knew that."

"I was a girl, remember?"

"That's no excuse." Danny grabbed a broom leaning against the wall and held it out to her.

She stared at it a second, then rolled her eyes, snatched it from him, and began to sweep up the remains of her pots. He watched her, remembering wood shop. The smell of sawdust and assorted toxic resins. The roar of the giant circular saw. The clenched jaw and icy blue eyes of the teacher, Mr. Mitchell, who had only nine and one-quarter fingers.

"Oh, hey," he said. "I made us a spare key for outside. I hid it under the Mateus bottle."

"Now that we have a spare we don't need the Mateus bottle, do we?"

"That's true," he acknowledged. "So where should I hide it?"

She thought it over. "I don't know."

"Me either. That's why I put it under the bottle."

"Makes sense, Rooms."

"That's what I thought, Rooms."

"G'night, Rooms."

"G'night, Rooms."

Their dinner of rice and beans had been eaten, the dishes and her Donovan albums put away. Those he would have to run over with his MG. She had taken her bath and now stood in his bedroom doorway in a cotton nightshirt, barefoot, slightly damp, fragrant. Jean Naté. Her smell. He was propped up on his bed, working on his report.

"Busy?" she asked shyly.

"Uh . . ." He put the papers down. "No."

"Just wanted to tell you I'm glad you're here."

"Me, too."

"I didn't realize it, but I've been lonesome. It's nice to have someone around again."

"Nice to be here."

He really ought to talk to Irv and Larry one more time about this executive committee idea. Exactly who belonged on it?

"You'll be leaving for work early?" she asked.

"Yes. Very."

And what about voting?

"I can get groceries," she offered.

"Swell. Need money?"

"You can pay me back. What do you think you'll want for dinner tomorrow night?"

Should Abe hold veto power?

"Um . . ."

"How about chicken?"

"Sounds good. Rooms, would you buy a reproduction art deco lamp?"

"I'd rather have an original."

"What if you couldn't afford one?"

"I'd wait until I could."

"Hmm."

"Unless it was really well made. That's what so nice about old things. The quality. No veneers or plastics. Otherwise, it might *look* nice, but inside it wouldn't be any nicer than—"

"The junk Pier West usually sells?"

"Uh-huh. G'night."

"Sleep tight, Rooms."

He heard her bedroom door close. Heard her bed springs creak. Thought of her long, slender golden body in the sheets. Thought of her next to him. Her hair tumbling across the pillow. Her breath soft and hot. The scent of her. Her fingers. Lips . . .

He stormed the kitchen. He could find only rice crackers and organic peanut butter. Personally Danny believed the secret ingredient in organic peanut butter was sand. Still he devoured the entire container and all of the rice crackers standing there in the kitchen.

He was not deceiving himself. He was helping a friend. She was broken. He was helping her put herself back together again. It would work. Sure it would.

Chapter Nine

"Pip, I have a new phone number."

She wrote it down in her memo pad.

"It's listed under the name of Rachel Stern," Danny added.

She raised her eyebrows. "Congratulations."

"It's platonic," he pointed out, lunging for a doughnut from the box on his desk. "So, did you read my report?"

"Yes, I did. I think it's the most exciting thing that's ever happened here. I'm . . . I'm proud to be associated with you."

"Thank you, Pip."

"Shall I type it up?"

"Please ask the Turks to come in first."

Danny sat back cautiously in his temperamental chair and put his hands behind his head. It *was* an exciting proposal. It laid the foundation for a company that embraced the best elements of profit incentive and social responsibility. He felt good about it.

Irv and Larry came in carrying their copies of the rough draft. Larry wore his aqua blue ensemble, Irv a broad grin.

"Close the door," Danny said. "Wait—ask Pip to come in, too. She's part of this."

She closed the door behind her, clearly pleased to be included. Danny offered doughnuts around. They declined. He didn't.

"We've worked on this together," Danny began, munching. "I've tried to take in everything. Make some sense of it. I just wanted to see if you thought anything was missing. Or off."

"I think it's a helluva report," Irv responded. "You've grasped the situation and made bold proposals."

"I'll second that," said Larry.

"Who do you think belongs on this governing board?" asked Danny. "Right now, I think it reads vague."

The Turks exchanged a look.

"All department heads?" ventured Larry.

"It's the only way to hear from everyone," mused Irv.

"Should the chairman have veto power?" asked Danny. "Or just one vote like everyone else?"

Larry lit a cigarette. "One vote."

"That seems unrealistic to me," countered Irv. "Mr. Levine presently rules with absolute authority. It'd be a major concession on his part just to *hear* from the staff."

"He'll never go for it," Pip said flatly.

Larry flushed. He didn't like for secretaries to speak, particularly against him.

"I agree with Pip," said Danny. "We have to consider the way the situation is now. This one vote thing, it's like a red flag."

"Of course, there's always the Straw Man theory," suggested Irv.

"Right," agreed Larry.

"That's true," admitted Pip.

They turned to Danny for his verdict.

"Exactly what is the Straw Man theory?" asked Danny.

"By leaving in one thing that's totally outrageous," answered Irv, "you protect something else controversial."

"So you think I should recommend one vote?" Danny asked Irv.

"Yes," Larry replied. "Definitely."

Irv took off his glasses and cleaned them on his tie. His eyes looked small and watery unprotected by the lenses. "I think you should do what you think is right."

"What do *you* think is right?" Danny pressed him.

"Any gain is a step in the right direction," Irv replied tactfully. "It's basically a question of how high you want to aim."

"You're ducking him, Green," snapped Larry.

"Calm down, Larry," Irv ordered. "We're here to offer advice. We shouldn't try to influence Danny in any particular direction. That would be overstepping our bounds."

"You're right," said Danny. "It's my report. I'm going to recommend one vote. I like this Straw Man theory. Besides, he said he wanted all my thoughts."

Irv said, "This new research and development department you suggest for getting us into manufacturing. Will it necessitate bringing in new people? Mr. Levine is against any idea that means—"

"We have the person to head it up right here," Danny said. "You."

Irv's eyes widened. "Wait, I don't like how this looks."

"How does it look?" asked Danny.

"Like I've been manipulating your report for my own gain."

"You haven't been," Danny assured him. "You're the right person for it. It's simple."

"Well . . . all right," Irv said reluctantly. "But that wasn't why I brought it up."

"I know that."

"And we'll all keep it in mind when we hand out the gold stars on Friday," concluded Larry drily as he got to his feet.

"Thanks again for your help, everybody," said Danny. "Pip'll clean it all up. You guys will be getting a copy."

They started out of his office.

"Irv? One more second?" asked Danny.

Irv remained. Larry left, irked at being excluded.

Danny reached for the last doughnut, bit into it. "How many miles did you say you run at lunch?"

Irv smiled. "Three. Care to join me?"

"I may," he replied. "My weight seems to be fluctuating a bit. Nerves, I guess." He chuckled heartily.

"Running's the best thing," Irv said, glancing at the empty doughnut box, "when you're hungry all the time."

"Maybe tomorrow."

"You got it." Irv started out, stopped. "Speaking of tomorrow, Charlene and I would like to have you over for dinner. We should get to know each other better. You should meet little Abraham."

"Love to."

"Great. Very casual, of course. Bring a lady."

"I'll do my best."

Pip finished typing up Danny's report at about two. It came to a dozen pages. He read it over one more time and signed it with a flourish. Then the personnel, associate chief of, took the rest of the day off.

He made it to Venice a little before four and stopped at B and B Hardware on Washington Boulevard, where he bought the longest-handled shovel in the place and a pair of Buddy Boy heavy-duty cotton work gloves.

Rachel's VW wasn't in the driveway. She was out. Good. Danny changed into jeans, a T-shirt, and work boots. Then he donned his new gloves and charged out back, long-handled shovel in hand.

It was still there, right next to the lettuce, its beady little eyes shut. It could almost be asleep. Jesus, what if it was? What if he woke it up?

Danny swallowed and retreated to the back fence. There he dug a good, proper hole. A solid foot deep.

Have to be dug eventually. May as well dig it now.
May as well make it two feet deep for that matter.

He forced himself to walk toward the garden. Closer.
Closer still. *Almost* close enough to touch it with the
shovel now, if he stretched. Such a teeny little thing,
really. He must have outweighed it by . . . well, no
point in going into that now. Closer. *There.* He nudged
it with the shovel. He touched it. He did. And it
didn't react at all. It was dead. It was definitely, for
sure, dead.

Danny heaved a big sigh, went inside, put on a long-
sleeved shirt, and drank a cold beer out of the bottle. A man's drink, for the man of the house.

He edged up close to it again, secure in the knowl-
edge that it was dead. A good idea, that intermedi-
ate step. Paid off. Because now . . . now he was *sssco-
ooooping* the shovel under it, his eyes shut tight. He
opened one a slit. Shit. Just got a shovel full of dirt.
He dumped it. C'mon, Big Dan. Again he *ssscoooooped.*
Squinted. Had it! Tail was dangling from the shovel
blade. *Moving.*

Eyes fastened on his good, proper hole, Danny
started across the yard. One step. Then another. God,
the hole seemed like it was in Reseda. There. He made
it. Dropped it in, his head turned away just like when
he used to get his polio vaccines from Dr. Goldman.
It nestled down into the hole. Quickly now, he covered it over with dirt. When the hole was filled he
tamped it down with the shovel. Then stood on it.
Then jumped up and down on it.

He did not mark the grave. He simply stowed his
shovel and work gloves in the studio and went inside and vomited. Then he brushed his teeth and went
back out with that day's *Wall Street Journal.* He never
thought he'd find himself reading the *Journal,* but they
did have some very interesting articles.

Rachel came home with groceries about a half-hour
later. She seemed cheerful. Danny helped her put

them away so she'd know he was willing to do his
share, and so he'd know where they were. He lit the
hibachi, and they sat out in the shade and drank some
wine while the coals got hot. He told her he had
turned in his report. She was pleased for him. He asked
her if she'd had a good day counseling at the abortion clinic.

"I had a frustrating day, actually," she replied. "The
laws . . . they infringe on personal freedom. They're
unfair. They ought to be changed. Only you have to
be a lawyer to get listened to."

"Does that mean Special Ed is out?"

"Why, don't you think law school's a good idea?"

It hit Danny. It actually hit him. At this moment—
the two of them sitting here in the shade, the smell
of charcoal lighter fluid in the air, the mouse safely
buried.

Rachel Stern wasn't perfect.

She was dizzy. She was vulnerable and mixed up and
more than a little mulish. She was *not perfect.*

He really hadn't believed her when she'd said so. To
him she *was* perfect—she just happened to be going
through a rough period. But now it hit him. This was
not, strictly speaking, a rough period. This was *her.*

Strangely, this realization made her seem even dearer
to him. More human. It made him feel strong. Use-
ful. Needed. He wanted to hold her and protect her.

"You don't think it's a good idea?" she repeated.

Danny swallowed some wine. "I think it's a real
good idea. If you really want to do it and can handle the workload. Some people can't."

"Ricky couldn't," she said quietly.

They sat there in silence for a second.

Suddenly she exclaimed, "Hey, the mouse is gone!"

"I buried it," Danny said offhandedly.

She smiled at him. Her old Malibu Rachel smile, with
dimples even. "I wanted to ask you to. I hate mice.
But I hate being a clinging female even more." She

reached across the picnic table and took his hand. "Thank you, Danny."

"No problem," he mumbled, his body turning to tapioca. "Just a dead thing. I've been meaning to take care of it."

"No, I owe you one. Really."

"Well, now that you mention it . . ."

"You sure I'm not too sloppy?"

They were on the freeway in the MG. Rachel was wearing white bib overalls. He had changed into jeans.

"Positive," he replied. "Irv said it was casual. Besides, you don't have to worry about making a good impression. *They* do."

"Is that because you're the boss's son?"

"Weird, huh?"

"Very."

"Would you think less of me if I told you I'm starting to like it?"

"I wouldn't believe you if you said you didn't. I really appreciate this, you coming."

"It'll be good for me. Force me to be sociable again."

Danny beamed. "That's the spirit."

Danny got off the freeway at La Brea and took it toward Hancock Park, which had been a very fancy neighborhood when Ev was in high school. Now mostly old people and young couples lived there. Irv and Charlene's street, Mansfield, was quiet and lined with trees. They lived on the top floor of a duplex. His and hers racing bicycles were parked in the hallway at the foot of the steps.

Irv had switched to jeans, too. He greeted Rachel with a warm smile and a handshake and gave Danny a signal of approval behind her back as he ushered them in.

The living room was airy and bare except for a worn leather sofa, an elaborate stereo, and a huge old At-

lantic Richfield Flying A electric sign, which took up
an entire wall. *Live Dead* by the Grateful Dead was
on the stereo.

"I love your sign," observed Rachel.

"Thanks," said Irv, pleased. "It was a complete mess
when I found it. Rewired it myself."

"Didn't you worry about getting electrocuted?" asked
Danny.

"There's a secret to that—wear rubber-soled shoes,
stand on a dry floor, and make sure your wife plugs
it in the first time."

They laughed.

Irv said, "Okay, let's get it out of the way. Hear
anything yet?"

"He wants to talk tomorrow. Pip scheduled an ap-
pointment. But I don't have any idea if he liked it."

"Nervous?"

"A little."

Irv clapped him on the back. "Don't be. You did a
great job."

"Couldn't have done it without you."

"Okay, Rachel," said Irv. "We won't discuss business any more. Deal?"

"Sounds good to me," said Danny.

"Ah, here's Charlene."

Charlene Green was short and round and intense. Her
bushy Afro was tinged with gray.

She shook Danny's hand, nearly pulling his arm out
at the socket. "Just so I don't make an ass of myself,
you two aren't married, right?"

"Right," said Rachel.

"But you live together?" asked Charlene.

"Right," said Danny.

"Join the club," said Irv. "We did that all through
college."

"How long have you been together?" asked Charlene.

"We're going on our second day," replied Rachel.

"And it's platonic," Danny pointed out.

Charlene frowned.

"That's very interesting," Irv said quickly. "Come and meet Abraham."

There was a dining room with a table set for four and a master bedroom crammed with books. The baby was asleep in his crib in the second bedroom. The four of them crowded into the doorway, watching him.

"Gee," whispered Danny. "A small human."

"He's a real person," whispered Irv. "A complete, fully-formed person. He has his own personality, tastes."

"Does he like Grand Funk Railroad?" whispered Danny.

"Has all their albums."

They started back toward the living room.

"He's totally changed our lives," said Charlene. "Before, all we cared about was work."

"Charlene's an urban planner," pointed out Irv.

"Now, we live around him," she said.

"Although it *is* very important for Charlene to keep working," said Irv. "And for me to take an active role in parenting. We don't want to be like the Cleavers."

"That's admirable," said Rachel.

"Mostly, it's hard," said Charlene.

They sat down on the sofa.

'Having a child really gives you a sense of responsibility for what we're doing to this world," said Irv. "You have a reason to care about what it'll be like after you're gone."

"It makes you think about things," added Charlene, as she poured them wine. "Like how we're going to live with Richard Nixon for four more years."

"You don't have to be a parent to worry about that," said Rachel.

"It could be worse," ventured Danny.

"How?" wondered Charlene.

"Ronald Reagan could be president."

They all laughed at the image of their governor sitting in the White House.

Irv shot a nervous glance over at his wife. "What would you folks say to . . . would you care to get high?"

"Would you be referring to something other than wine?" asked Danny, deadpan.

"Yes, I would," Irv replied, deadpan. "One down. Nine to Rachel."

"Would this be a controlled substance?" she asked, playing along gamely.

"Yes, it would."

"Would it be . . . *marijuana*?" asked Danny.

"Yes, it would."

"Sounds good to me," said Danny.

"Whew. Good," said Irv, relieved. He produced a joint and lit it. "Felt funny asking, but I figured . . ."

"Sure, sure," said Danny, taking the joint. "I sort of figured you did, too. Kind of weird, though, getting stoned with somebody you know from the office."

"That's right, you're new to it. It takes a little getting used to."

"Nice, smooth dope," said Danny, passing the joint to Rachel.

"Know where you can get some."

"I'll keep it in mind."

Rachel took a polite toke and passed it along to Charlene, who declined.

"Mind if I ask you an urban planning question?" Danny said to Charlene.

"This should be interesting," she said. "Go ahead."

"What can we do about the freeway traffic? It's *impossible* to get around anymore."

"That's L.A.," she said simply. "They won't plan. Won't agree to a moratorium on growth. Won't consider mass transit. The only thing I can suggest is staggering your company's work day. That way your employees can use the freeways at quieter hours."

"That's a good idea," said Danny.

"Anything beats the Santa Ana Freeway at 5:30," agreed Irv.

"We oughta draw up a plan."

"I think you should try to do more," argued Rachel.

"Such as?" asked Irv.

"Such as whatever you can," she replied.

"I like this person," said Charlene.

"I take it you think it's the role of business to influence public policy," Irv asked her, leaning forward.

"Yes, I do."

"Even if that business influence could be a negative one?" he said. "Like, say, the influence that's gotten us into Vietnam?"

"Look, it's there," said Rachel. "It exists. It's up to guys like you to counteract it."

"You mean, donate support to the anti-war movement?" asked Danny.

"Yes. Absolutely."

"Hmm. That's a very interesting point you're making, Rachel," said Irv. "I couldn't agree with you more. The ethics of business is fascinating, and much ignored. We don't exist in a vacuum, like people tend to believe. We affect the lives of everyone who walks into our stores. That carries a responsibility. Nobody talks about it much. But they're going to start talking about it, now that it's getting to be our turn. Right, Danny?"

Danny grinned. "Right."

It was true. If he stuck it out, it wouldn't be long before he'd actually be in charge of Pier West. *Running things.* Running them the right way. Other companies would follow his example. City governments. State governments . . . *Greed will end. A new day will dawn. That, Daniel, is what I will be doing.*

"Kind of a trip, huh?" Irv was saying to him.

"Y-yeah. A trip."

"It should be," Irv declared enthusiastically, hand-ing him the joint. "If you can get high on business, you can get ahead in it."

"I hope you two like pizza," Charlene said.

"She makes it from scratch," Irv pointed out.

"There's salad, too. Cesar Chavez personally blessed the lettuce."

"Sounds wonderful," said Rachel.

"Can we do anything?" asked Danny.

"You can sit," Charlene ordered. "You're our guests."

The two of them headed off to the kitchen. Danny relaxed into the cushions.

"Nice couple," he said.

"Uh-huh."

"It's good to be working with someone like him. Someone who thinks like we do. She's nice, too. And they even like each other. Kind of reassuring. I've been starting to think Mouse and Wendy are the norm." He glanced over at her. She was gazing at the Flying A sign. She had that same sad, distant look on her face she had at the wedding reception. Danny hesitated, almost reached over and touched her arm. "You okay, Rooms?"

She shuddered. "Yes. I'm . . . I'm sorry, Danny. I haven't been . . . haven't felt like part of a couple in a while. It's freaking me out a little."

"Don't much like it, huh?"

"That's not it. The problem is, I do."

Chapter Ten

"Come in, kiddo. Sit, sit."

Danny sat stiffly in the chair facing Abe's desk, his back to the glassed warehouse wall. On the desk lay Danny's report, marked in various places.

Abe was in an expansive mood. He seemed pleased. "I want you to know how proud I am of you. You've worked very hard at this. It shows."

Danny let his breath out, relieved. "Thanks, Pop."

"I'm the one who should be saying thanks. Kiddo?"

"Yes, Pop?"

"Thanks." Abe leaned back in his chair and put his feet up on his desk. Funny, he seemed to have no problem with *his* chair. "As I see it, there's really only one problem with your report, kiddo. One small problem: Pier West is headquartered in La Mirada, California. Not in *Minsk*."

Danny felt himself sinking in his chair. "What do you mean?"

"I mean, *comrade*, that every idea in here either costs me money or qualifies as outright socialism."

"C-can you be specific?"

"Sure. I'll be specific." Abe put his glasses on his

nose and began thumbing through the report. He stopped. "I'll quote you: 'Problem—High employee turnover at retail outlets, as well as pilfering and low productivity.' A definite problem, kiddo. I agree. 'Solution—At present, all Pier West retail employees except for managers and assistant managers are paid minimum hourly wages and receive no benefits. I propose all outlets be staffed exclusively by full-time salaried employees, who will receive full health coverage as well as participate in a profit-sharing plan to be worked out for each outlet. Employees will thus have a greater stake in the profitability of their stores. They will stay. They will work harder.' "

"*I'd* work harder," argued Danny.

"You also happen to understand the concept of work. A lot of these people—"

"You get what you pay for, Pop. Right now, you pay—"

"Very little. And I intend to keep it that way. I also don't intend to turn this company into some kind of goddamned welfare agency."

"Can you be—?"

"Specific? Absolutely. Here: 'Employee benefit reorganization—As this company grows, it must accept a greater responsibility for the quality of the lives of its employees, their families, and the community they live in. To this end, I propose Pier West management draw up plans for an employee credit union, a company-run day care center for single mothers, and a college scholarship fund for employees and their children. I further propose a mandatory hiring quota for minorities and the handicapped. I was shocked to find that only eight percent of present salaried employees are minorities, and of those, over eighty percent work as secretaries or warehousemen. The remainder are employed in the stores. With one notable exception, none are in La Mirada front office positions. I further propose the creation of an employee review board, to be made up equally by management and non-management members, to enforce these personnel quotas, as well as examine and approve all layoffs and firings.' " Abe put the report back down on his desk. "Kiddo, let me explain something—if I do these things, I won't make any money."

"You've definitely got problems here, Pop. And I think they boil down to one simple thing—you have to start thinking more about the people who work here than about how much money you make."

"Ah, that's where you're wrong!" exclaimed Abe. "I *am* thinking about them." He pointed to the warehousemen on the other side of the glass. "If I don't make money they don't work. It's as 'simple' as that. Besides, it's your money, too. Keep that in mind."

"I am."

"I don't think so. If you were you'd be thinking more like a businessman than a college kid."

Danny felt himself heating up inside.

"A businessman don't give up what he already has," said Abe. "Like with this . . ." He hunted through the report. "Here. 'Problems: Poor front office morale. Lack of opportunity for advancement. Major decision-making bottlenecks at the top.' " Abe peered at Danny over his glasses. "By 'the top' I assume you mean me," he said drily.

"That's correct."

"Right. 'Solution—A governing board composed of the president and all the department heads, each with one vote. The board will vote on policy decisions, as well as insure better front office input and communication. The president should also consider offering share-holding in the company as an incentive to secure the long-term commitment of top-flight management employees.' Okay. First of all, I don't believe in meetings. Just a bunch of people sitting around in a room doing nothing. Second, it's *my* company. I'm not gonna submit my ideas to some goddamned board.

Third of all, I don't care if people in the front office are unhappy. They're always gonna be unhappy. Fourth, I don't care if they leave. People are always gonna leave. The only constant is us. You and me."

"Pop, you have to delegate authority. You're losing top people. Bright people."

"Let 'em go. I didn't need 'em to build the company and I don't need 'em to keep us on top."

"You *do*! You're a great businessman. I don't dispute that. What I'm saying here in this report . . . what I'm trying to say is you have to start thinking bigger."

"Don't tell me how to run my business!" barked Abe.

"You *asked* me to!"

"That's true," Abe admitted. "All right, go ahead, tell me how to run my business."

"Okay. Like with my proposal to start an R and D department geared toward manufacturing your own merchandise. You've been advised repeatedly to do it. You should, and you won't. Why not?"

"There's an old, old saying in business, kiddo—"

" 'If it ain't broken, don't fix it.' I know that one. There's also another one: 'If you're not moving forward you're a target.' "

"If I'd known you were gonna use it against me I'd never have told it to ya," Abe said sourly.

"I'm not against you. I'm with you. Only, you have to face the facts. The business has changed. You're not . . ." Danny trailed off.

"I'm not what?"

"You're not Moss Stationery anymore," Danny said quietly.

"You think I don't know that?"

"I think you're a target. Import Barn is cutting into your market, undercutting your prices. You can't keep stocking the stores with close-outs. You *have* to manufacture yourself."

"We don't know how to do it," Abe said.

"We'll learn."

Abe grinned. " 'We'?"

Danny's breath caught. He'd never referred to the company that way before. Just sort of spilled out of him. "Y-you need better organization," he went on, a little rattled. "The stores don't even know what merchandise the other stores have in stock. They should all be hooked up to a central computer."

"I've been intending to do that," conceded Abe, still grinning at him. "I'll follow up on that."

"What about the rest?"

Abe's smile disappeared. "Unrealistic. Out of the question."

"You're wrong."

"I'm the boss. It's my decision to make. When you're the boss, it'll be your decision. And you'll see it a lot differently than you do now, believe me."

"Nothing's changed, has it. You still know everything. I'm still a little—"

"That's not true, kiddo."

"A lot of time and thought and work went into these proposals. You have to respect them."

"I do respect them. It's not a question of respect. It's a question of right and wrong. I'm right and you're wrong. And don't make the mistake of personalizing this thing. I'm only telling you what any boss at any company would tell you."

"This isn't any company. This is a family business. That's what you always told me. I'm a member of the family. I want to do these things."

"No, you don't. You think you do, but you don't. Listen to me. I know best at this point, okay? I'm protecting your interests. You don't want to give away shares. Give away control. It's suicide. Somebody has to be in charge. Right now, it's me. Someday it'll be you. And on that day you'd be awful darned sorry if I'd saddled you with a bureaucracy, with red tape,

with a bunch of jerks you couldn't get rid of. You'd
never be able to get anything done. I know what I'm
talking about. You're just out of the chute. You got
your whole lifetime here. Relax." Abe closed his report and pushed it aside. "Tell you what. Sit down
with Irving and start outlining this American Heritage
series. It's your baby."

"I want to follow up on these proposals. Okay,
maybe we can't do all of them. Maybe that's unrealistic. I'm willing to compromise."

"We're not gonna do any of 'em, kiddo. The matter is closed."

"Then I'm leaving personnel."

"Don't be a hothead. You made a commitment and
you're sticking to it. You don't quit just because you
don't get your way. That's childish. Besides, what
would I tell Mom?"

"Now who's personalizing this?"

"You agreed to work here for one year," stated Abe,
stabbing his desk blotter with his index finger for
emphasis.

"I know. But I didn't stipulate where. I'd like to
serve the balance of the year in the warehouse, earn-
ing whatever wage the other warehousemen—"

"No!"

Danny stood up. "It's that or I quit outright."

"For where?" Abe demanded.

"Anywhere. I'm spontaneous."

Abe let out a short, harsh laugh. They glared at each
other across the desk. Finally Abe tossed his pen
away, disgusted.

"Fine. Go move crates. Be a stubborn jerk."

"Maybe I am a stubborn jerk—"

"There's no maybe to it."

"I had no choice—it's an inherited trait."

Danny stormed out of The Czar's office.

★   ★   ★

"I haven't been this sorry about anything in ages,"
said Irv, genuinely crushed.

"Me either," agreed Larry glumly.

"We tried," said Danny trying to cheer them up,
though he didn't much feel like it himself. "That's
all a person can do. I guess you guys will be leaving,
huh?"

"Good chance," acknowledged Larry. "Damned good
chance."

"Well," said Danny. "Don't be strangers. Any time
you need a carload of scented candles, you know who
to see."

They tried to smile, but they were too disappointed.
Same with Pip. She stayed in Danny's office after they
left, chewing on her lower lip.

Danny began to clean out his desk. "Sure sorry to
leave you in the lurch like this, Pip. Mr. Bell is going
to need a new secretary for a while, isn't he? Rosalyn
is leaving to have her baby."

Pip said, "Something tells me this whole thing will
blow over in a day or two."

Danny closed the desk drawer, looked around at what
had been his office. "You really think so?"

"You're the heir. He can't afford to lose you."

"He lost me."

For his final act as personnel, associate chief of,
Danny removed several of the multicolored stick pins
in the map of the West Coast and stuck them in places
where they didn't belong.

"I don't get it, man," confessed Bobby Clarke, the
red-bearded warehouse manager. "You're gonna be
workin' for *me*?"

They stood out on the warehouse floor, surrounded
by noise and activity and music. The radio was blaring something new by Jefferson Starship. Danny vastly
preferred them when they were the Airplane. Then,
it had been music.

He nodded. "And I want to be treated like everybody else."

"But you're Mr. Levine's—"

"No favors. I screw up, you kick my ass. Okay?"

"Okay," Bobby said reluctantly. "You operate a
forklift?"

"I can learn."

"We'll get you goin' on that tomorrow." Bobby
looked him over. "You might wanna wear different
clothes. For now—ya see that there pile of crates?"

"Yes, I do."

"You move what's in that pile to that truck. Tito
and Raoul'll load it. Mr. Levine, I sure feel strange
about this."

"It's Danny. And don't. By the way, a lot of the
guys may not know who I am. I'd like it if it stays
that way."

"They won't hear it from me."

Danny took off his jacket and tie and rolled up his
sleeves. Then he shook hands with Tito and Raoul
and got started hoisting, carrying, grunting, *working*.
Good, hard, honest work like the kind he did in the
fields outside Salinas.

The only bad part was when he glanced at the glass
wall between the warehouse and Abe's office. Abe
stood watching him, hands on his hips.

Danny noticed his lower back, shoulders, and arms
were giving out somewhere around three o'clock. He
also noticed pairs of guys occasionally heading for the
john together, dragging on tired legs, only to emerge
a few minutes later, grinning. Marijuana, Danny suspected, was being smoked in there. Even Bobby went
in there once. Here was yet another reason for poor
employee productivity, one he hadn't even thought
to include in his report: Everyone in the warehouse,
including its manager, was stoned.

Most of his major muscle groups ached by the time
he got home, and both hands quivered from exhaus-

tion. Strange cars were parked outside. Inside, Rachel was seated at the kitchen table with a bunch of women.

"This is my housemate, Danny," she told them. "Danny, these are my friends from the abortion clinic. We're putting some thoughts together on how to link up with the other independent clinics in the city. This is Gloria, Audrey, Diane . . ."

Danny kept right on walking toward the back door, the bag holding his supper tucked under his arm.

"Danny?!" she called after him.

He went out the door, flopped down on the back steps, and pulled out his family-size bag of Wampum corn chips and his six-pack of Coors. He sure didn't feel like talking to anybody.

By the time he finished his fourth beer his muscles were getting numb and he was crunching the handy new pop-top cans in his fist and heaving them out into the garden like grenades. After his fifth he imitated the sound of an explosion when the grenade landed and called out huskily, "Two more dead Jerries, Sarge!"

Too bad Newt wasn't around. He felt like a to-the-death lemon fight. There was a tree right next door full of 'em. Possibly he could persuade the abortion caucus to engage in combat. Nah. Girls cried when you hit 'em. Besides, he could hear car doors closing now and engines starting. And the back door was opening behind him.

Rachel was out there with him now. He turned to look up at her. His stiffening neck punished him for it.

"Want a beer?" he offered, wincing.

She poked at the empty plastic six-pack rings with her sandal. "There aren't any left."

"I can go get some more."

"No, thank you." She sat down next to him on the steps. Briefly their thighs touched. She withdrew hers. "I don't mean to be critical, but you could have been a little more supportive."

"Supportive?"

"I made a real effort tonight. I reached out, met with people for the first time in months. It was a real positive step for me. And all you did was growl and run out here. You didn't even say hello."

Danny drained his last beer, crunched it, and heaved it off into the darkness with the others. *"Kapowwwwwww . . ."*

"Danny, what's wrong?"

He shrugged. "Just business."

"Don't be such a fucking Jewish male," she snapped.

"Who's being a fucking Jewish male?" he demanded.

"You are. Jewish men just love to talk to women about their sinuses and their bowels and their sexual hang-ups. But as soon as it has to do with work or money you totally clam up."

"Big Rick had sexual hang-ups?"

"Tell me what's wrong."

"You don't want to hear about it."

"I do, too, damn it."

"Okay, okay. My pop . . . he sort of blew his nose on my report. I sort of quit over it. I'm in the warehouse now."

She stared at him, shocked. "Danny, you can't just give up like that."

"I didn't give up. I took a stand."

"You walked away from the fight. What kind of stand is that? So maybe you had a setback. You still have to stick it out."

"I've been thinking I might hit the road again, actually."

"Running away never solves anything."

"You know, people always say that, but I was a lot happier when I was avoiding this. All I had to worry about then was my next ride, my next meal."

"That's not life. That's survival."

"Most people are very content with that."

"We're not most people."

"Look, I'm really not in the mood to hear this."

"Tough," she snapped.

He looked at her, surprised by her vehemence. Her eyes shone in the light from the kitchen. She seemed genuinely upset.

"Well . . . I'm not going anywhere tonight except bed," Danny assured her. "If I can make it that far." He struggled to his feet with a groan. His back was bent from all of the lifting, and his arms hung low at his side like Magilla Gorilla's. "Maybe I'll take a hot shower."

"There's some stir fry left."

"Thanks, I'm not hungry."

"You *are* upset."

He glowered down at her.

"You better be nice to me or I won't give you a backrub."

"You gonna give me a backrub?"

She nodded.

"Gee. What a pal." He started inside, stopped. "You think I should go on a diet?"

"I think if you took off about twenty pounds you'd have to beat them off with a stick."

"I would?"

"And I'd be very jealous."

"You would?"

"I'd lose you. A good roomy is hard to find."

Danny signed inwardly. "What else do I need to do?"

"Seriously? Mmm . . . Learn how to flirt. You're a little sincere."

"I thought sincere was an asset."

"Oh, it is. Only, it's also a little safe. And for a woman safe is . . . Remember you were talking about your fear? The one that was like being locked in a closet? Safe is like that."

He yawned again. "Gotcha. Thanks, Rooms."

"You're welcome, Rooms."

"And to think your brother said this wouldn't work."

"He did? How come?"

"He said it's impossible for two people to live to-gether platonically if one of them has a . . . a . . ."

"Has a what?"

"I'm gonna go take my shower now."

The hot water felt good. He could have soaked in it for hours, only it started turning cold in minutes. A definite disadvantage to living in an old shack. Still, his muscles felt looser when he flopped down on his bed on his stomach, wearing a clean T-shirt and cut-offs.

Rachel kneeled, leaned her flank into him, and be-gan to work her lovely fingers into his shoulders.

"Feel good?" she asked.

He tried to answer her but managed only to drool into his pillow. He turned his head to one side. "Was tonight's meeting productive?"

"We got a petition together. But I keep thinking how tired I am of this grass roots stuff."

"Still thinking about law school?"

She began to work her hands down his spine. "I have the grade point average."

"And you're a woman. They want women now."

She hit the small of his back, which was totally bunched. He groaned.

"You've also got terrific hands," he added. "That's very important in the legal profession."

"What are you talking about, silly?"

"I'm practicing my flirting. You don't mind, do you?"

"No, I suppose not. Just warn me next time."

He began to feel weak all over. She kneaded one arm, then the other. Each one fell onto the bed next to him, dead. He felt as if he was floating on a raft now, drifting, drifting . . . And as he slipped away the bed-room light went out, and it was dark, and he thought he felt cool lips on his forehead, but he was fairly certain he dreamt that part.

★   ★   ★

"Main thing to remember about a forklift is know where you are at all times," said Bobby.

Danny nodded. "Know where you are. Right." He wore a flannel shirt, jeans, and workboots his second day in the warehouse. His Buddy Boy work gloves were tucked in his back pocket. He had not shaved.

"Know where your co-workers are," Bobby went on. "Watch your back. Familiarize yourself with the equipment. This ain't no toy. It's a piece of serious work equipment. That means no hot-rodding. Not that you need to be reminded of that, Mr. Levine."

"Danny."

He climbed aboard. There was one forward gear, one reverse gear. The lift was controlled by a lever. It seemed simple enough.

And it was. In no time at all Danny was deftly lifting giant skids of crates, zipping them across the warehouse floor, and lowering them onto the truck beds. Tommy and Freddy were on the beds today. They both had ponytails and fuzzy faces and permanent stoner grins, and didn't know about Danny's family connection. He felt sure of this because of what they nicknamed him.

"Over here, Porky!" called Tommy, waving him to the bed.

"Nice and easy, Pork," added Freddy, guiding him. "Nice and easy . . ."

A little before lunch Danny noticed Tommy and Freddy drifting into the john together. He decided it was time to take firm action on this situation. He climbed down from the forklift, pocketed his work gloves, and followed them.

They were crouched in one of the stalls with the door closed and cigarettes going to cover up the smell. Nobody else was in there.

Danny cleared his throat and tapped on the closed stall door. "Guys?"

"Who is it?" Tommy asked nervously.

"Danny," he replied.

"Who?" Freddy demanded.

"Uh . . . Porky."

"Hey, why didn't ya say so? Come on in, Pork. Always room for one more."

They opened the stall door and made room for him. It was a tight fit and a little warm but they weren't there for comfort. Freddy handed him the joint. He drew on it. Then he passed it to Tommy.

"Kind of like high school, huh?" Danny observed, scratching his stubbled cheeks.

"Better than high school," said Tommy.

"The Czar's *payin'* us to get high," said Freddy.

"Nice work if you can get it," grinned Danny.

"We got it, dude," said Tommy.

They dissolved into laughter.

"Great seats, huh?"

"Great."

The seats were four rows behind the Dodger dugout. They were Larry's seats. Danny and Irv were parked in them, munching on Dodger Dogs. Larry sat by himself out by the left field foul pole in a general admission seat. It occurred to Danny that this was a little odd, but it didn't bother him. He had been stoned all day.

It was a treat being back in the Stadium again. Green grass. White uniforms. Short-haired fathers and sons. Thrifty Mexican families. Helen Dell playing "Take Me Out to the Ball Game" on the organ. It was as if time had stopped here. The only difference was a lot of the players were now Danny's own age. This Phillies pitcher, Carlton, could throw.

"So how are you enjoying the warehouse?" Irv asked.

"Why, thinking of making a move?"

Irv laughed. "Just wondered how you felt. We didn't get a chance to talk."

Danny finished his last Dodger Dog and dropped the

wrapper on the cement between his feet. "To tell you the truth, I think it was probably the best thing that could have happened."

"You do?" asked Irv, surprised.

"I do. See, I was getting emotionally involved in the company. It's better this way."

"You're not angry?"

"It's his company."

"Well, Larry and I are upset. For your sake and for ours. We believe in Pier West. We want to grow with it." Irv glanced over at him, tugged at his beard thoughtfully. "It doesn't have to be this way, Danny. There's another avenue the three of us can pursue, so you won't be wasted back there on the floor."

"I don't feel wasted," Danny assured him. "What avenue?"

The little kid right behind Danny blew his stadium horn in Danny's ear. Danny resisted the urge to grab the horn and break it over his knee.

"As it stands," Irv said, "there doesn't seem to be a viable solution on the horizon. Mr. Levine is only fifty-eight. Retirement is—"

"He'll never retire. You'll have to carry him out on a stretcher. What avenue?"

"You'd have to get actively involved," Irv warned him.

"If you want me to talk to him again, I will. But I don't think it'll do much good."

"I don't either. What Larry and I have in mind is, well, we've been talking to some people who can lay their hands on capital."

"You want to buy the company? Forget it. He'll never sell."

"We want to buy your half."

Danny froze. "*My* half?"

"If we were partners he'd have to listen to us. He'd have no choice."

"But I'm a partner now," said Danny. "He doesn't listen to me."

"It's different when it's outside money."

"You mean . . . squeeze him out?"

"Not at all. I don't think that's the case. I've been giving it a lot of thought, from the standpoint of ethics, and my honest feeling is he'll be a lot better off—he and the company and all of its employees. Times have changed. The man's in over his head. This way, he can save face, hold on to a title, some authority. He just won't have *sole* authority. You'll move into a front office position. You, me, and Larry. His Young Turks. We'll run Pier West together. Move it forward, like we want to. We're ready."

"He's my father, Irv."

"I know that. Believe me."

"I mean, you're making it sound like it's . . ."

"Like it's what?"

Danny took a deep breath, let it out slowly. "Possible."

"It's very possible."

"Who would you raise the money from?"

"A reputable source. There's nothing shady. This isn't about money. It's about control, the kind we don't have now. It's about responsibility. Your responsibility."

"What makes you think I'd do something like this?"

"We're betting on your foresight."

"You're also betting I won't call him up tonight and tell him about this, aren't you?"

"I suppose we are," Irv admitted.

"Well, that part's pretty safe," Danny confessed. "He and I aren't exactly on friendly terms right now. Look, Irv, I'm going to have to think this over."

"Of course. There's no pressure. We've got a few weeks to let the investors know. Give it some thought. Think about what the three of us can do with Pier West. And think about you."

"What about me?"

"You aren't the sort of guy who backs away from a fight. Hides."

"I'm not?"

"You're your father's son."

"Gee, I wish you hadn't said that."

"I mean it in a flattering way, Danny."

"I still wish you—"

"I respect your father. He's a great seat-of-his-pants operator. Only, this is the corporate age. This is *our* time. We're the new generation, and we've got something to say."

Danny frowned. "Wasn't that the Monkees' theme song?"

Irv grinned. "I thought it sounded familiar."

"I'll think it over, Irv."

"Great. And I want you to know, whatever you decide to do, we're with you." Irv stood up. "I'll see you after the game."

"Where are you going? It's only the third inning."

"I'm going to switch seats with Larry. He hates sitting so far away. I couldn't care less. I'll let you in on a little secret—I hate baseball."

Chapter Eleven

Abe didn't look up from the grease spot he was scrubbing. He was in the driveway on his knees, wearing baggy old slacks, a torn undershirt, and sneakers that had once belonged to Danny—his Saturday afternoon outfit.

"Ya believe it?!" he barked. "I told the stupid sonuvabitch to park in the *street!*"

"Which stupid sonuvabitch?" asked Danny, clutching his pile of dirty laundry.

"Aw, that goddamned dishwasher repairman. Left his goddamned truck in the driveway and now I've got grease spots all over the goddamned place." Abruptly, Abe stopped his scrubbing and peered up at Danny with narrowed eyes. "What do *you* want?"

"I came to see Mom," Danny replied sharply. "That okay?"

"See whoever you want. What do I care?"

Danny started for the front door. Coco sat on the steps, leashed to the doorknob.

"Only she ain't here, kiddo."

Danny stopped. "Where is she?"

"Her Jewish Center, playing with her books. They

all get Jewisher when they get old. She went to *shul*
this morning, ya believe it? And now she wants me to
take her to Israel. Can you see me in Israel?"

"Yes, I can."

"Screw you, too." Abe resumed scrubbing, a bit
more vigorously than before. "Leave the laundry on
the steps."

"That's okay. I'll take it to a laundromat."

"Put it down! No sense *shlepping* it all the way to
the goddamned Center just so the old lady'll have to
shlep all the way back here. I'm thinking of her."

"Well, seeing as how you put it that way."

Coco had a new greeting for Danny—she turned her
back on him. He deposited the laundry next to her,
hesitated, then moved it a little farther away from her.

Abe tossed his scrub brush in the bucket next to him.
"Grab me that hose, will ya?"

Danny fetched it. Abe got to his feet with a groan,
snatched it from him. They glared at each other in
silence, stalemated. Neither of them could talk. Not
about this.

This was *tsuris*.

The Jewish Community Center was on Olympic just
past Midway Hospital on Fairfax. Danny hadn't been
back to this neighborhood since that night he flipped
out on "windowpane" and drove off in quest of the
old lady who kept the talking horse in her back yard.
He'd ended up spending half the night in a driveway, weeping, as Mister Ed told him what a no-
good, worthless, stoned-out bum he was. The next
morning he realized he'd been dressed down by a basketball hoop. He was lucky. Lucky he'd survived.

How could Newt still do it?

Ev was behind the desk in the small library. Danny
considered pretending he was checking out a book
so that when she looked up she'd get a real surprise.
But he thought better of it—he had no smelling salts
with him.

So he simply said "*Shalom*, Mom," in a loud, clear voice so as not to startle her.

And she simply said "Sssh!"

Outside there was a small patio with benches and a mosaic tile mural depicting the Jews being led off to the death camps.

"Cheery scene," observed Danny.

"It's very important for people to remember, sweetheart."

"How can they forget? We're constantly reminding them."

"Want tea?"

"Okay."

"There's cake."

"No, thanks. I'm trying to cut down." Danny sat. "What kind of cake?"

"Marble."

"Maybe a sliver."

In the chair next to Danny an old, old man was snoring, his nose dripping. On the other side of the fence there was a playground where a short, muscular young woman was leading a calisthenics class of little old ladies in sweatsuits.

Ev returned with two steaming Styrofoam cups and Danny's cake on a napkin. He bit into the cake. It tasted like it was made from matzo meal left over from Passover, 1957.

"Mind if I ask you something delicate?" Danny began.

Ev smiled. "Don't be concerned about delicate with me. I'm the one who taught you how to wipe out your little tushie, remember?"

Danny reddened. "That was a while ago."

"That was yesterday, mister."

"It's about the business. Has Pop . . . Has he ever considered selling?"

"He's had offers."

"And . . . ?"

"They weren't good enough. It wasn't the money. The money was always fine. It was the terms."

"What terms?"

"They wouldn't guarantee you a spot."

The cake seemed even drier now. "Is that so important?"

"It is to him. Do you know what he said to me after he turned down the last offer? 'Let those schmucks start their own family business.' Besides, what would he do if he sold out? He doesn't play golf. He doesn't sail. He's never even taken a vacation. Not once since the day we were married."

The calisthenics class broke up. Three little boys in bermuda shorts and yarmulkes dribbled a basketball out onto the court and began to play two-on-one.

"Play him tight, Ira!" screamed one. *"Tighter!"*

"Dad isn't entirely against your proposals, you know," Ev said.

"He isn't?"

"He knows he needs to make changes. He wants to say yes to some of them."

"Which ones?"

"Only, he's afraid."

"Pop?"

"Yes, Pop. He's afraid of change. Afraid of tampering with success. Afraid. It's not something he could ever admit to you, or even to me. But there it is."

"Change is how you stay a success, isn't it? That's what he always used to say."

"Sweetheart, it's easy to say. He's number one in his field. It's the competition who are supposed to scramble, not him."

"I'm talking about making the company more responsible for its employees, Mom."

"That part he doesn't have much problem with."

"Then what is he—?"

"The manufacturing business."

"But *everybody* says it's the right way to go."

"He knows that. He's known it for years."

"So why hasn't he done anything?"

Ev looked at him with a puzzled expression on her face. "You really don't get it, do you?"

"Get what?"

"Why he turned you down."

"He said I was being unrealistic."

Ev shook her head. "I don't intend to get caught in the middle of this. I won't take sides. Let me just say this—the things you proposed, a lot of them are very fine ideas. But they're not easy. And they can't all be done at once. It may take twenty years. Your father, *he isn't going to be around then.* You have yet to give him the slightest assurance that you're pre-pared to shepherd your proposals through after he's gone. You haven't told him you're going to *stay.*"

Danny swallowed. *Twenty years?* "Oh," he said hoarsely.

"One of the things Judaism teaches you is patience," Ev said. "Always there are the extremists. The Jerry Rubins. The H. Rap Browns. They want sweeping change, and they want it today. But meaningful, fun-damental change takes a long, long time. The middle ground has to shift, and it shifts very slowly."

"Maybe it has to get kicked in the pants once in a while."

"Maybe," she conceded. "But the person in charge has to weigh *all* points of view. Reach a sound, care-ful decision. Right or wrong, what he decides will af-fect all of those other people."

"Gee, Mom, all I want is to do some good for the company."

"And what good are you doing by working in the warehouse?"

Danny began to examine his shoes.

"If you didn't want to hear that you wouldn't have come here," she pointed out. "Or did you just come to bring me your laundry?"

"I have no laundry with me," he answered truthfully.

"I have another question."

Danny sighed. "Yes, Mom, I'm taking good care of myself."

"That wasn't my question. What's going on with Rachel Stern?"

"Nothing. It's platonic, like I told you."

"You know it's a sin to try to fool a mother, particularly your own."

"Jews don't have sins. We don't need them." Danny took her hand. There were liver spots on it. He patted it. "It's fine."

Jenny Biddle was the only woman Danny knew who could no doubt beat the shit out of him if she wanted to. Newt's kid sister stood six feet tall in her heavy black motorcycle boots, and she weighed close to 200 pounds, most of it meat. She was tuning her Norton Commando in the concrete driveway in front of their garage. Wrenches, parts, and lubricating fluids were arrayed on the pavement next to her. Danny watched her there for a second, amazed as he often was by just how much she and Newt looked alike. Same even blue eyes, tangled blond hair, patrician nose, cleft chin, upturned upper lip. She paused to wipe the sweat from her forehead with the back of a greasy hand. It was then that she spotted Danny standing there clutching his six-pack of Dos Equis and bagful of machaca burritos from Burrito King, the little stand on Sepulveda.

"My God, it's Daniel!" she exclaimed. "It's been *ages!*"

"Hey, Jen. How have you been?"

She wiped her hands on a rag and gave him a bear hug and didn't let go for a second. Hers was a sweet nature, actually, once you got past the Hell's Angels wardrobe.

"Newt had to go out for a minute," she said. "Go

get the opener while I wash up. I was hoping you'd come around. Been wanting to talk to you."

The teenaged girl Danny had seen a few weeks before sitting on the front steps staring at an album cover was now sitting at the kitchen table staring at the wall. She was not wearing any trousers, and a cigarette was burning down unsmoked in her fingers. Danny took it from her and put it out. She didn't react. Her fingers were cold.

A corncob was going around in the living room, and *Abbott and Costello Meet Frankenstein* was blaring away on the TV. The windows were closed, the shades drawn. It was darker and stuffier than Danny remembered, and it smelled like a laundry hamper. Shanny, a feisty, beady-eyed little freak Danny had never liked, was intently playing Monopoly with Rebel, a tall, bearded redhead who liked to keep a Bowie knife handy in a sheath on his belt. Oly, a very timid philosophy grad student whose father was a Lutheran minister, sat on the sofa reading *One Flew Over the Cuckoo's Nest* and listening to music on the headphones. A young couple Danny didn't recognize were stretched out on the rug reading Zap Comix and absently stroking each other's erogenous zones. All of them were oblivious to Danny as he stood there in the doorway. He felt like he was watching animals in a zoo cage. It hadn't been so long ago that he'd been one of them—hanging out, zonked, totally convinced he was making some kind of meaningful statement. Now all he could think of was how uneasy he felt standing there, and how glad he was he'd left.

The warm grease from the machaca burritos had soaked through the bottom of the bag and was running down his arm and onto his pants. He found the opener and went back outside.

Jenny was scrubbing her hands with a bar of Lava in the big garage sink. The garage hadn't changed. Newt's king-sized water bed still sat in the center like

an island, scarred wooden Adirondack chairs fanned
around it. Brick and board shelves held his TV and
stereo, the urn with Mrs. Biddle's ashes in it, and
Newt's books. Newt owned hundreds and hundreds
of science fiction paperbacks—the kind with pictures
of large, distasteful insects on the cover. Fantasy, he
believed, broadened one's horizons. Overhead, ply-
wood was stretched across the rafters to hold whatever was left from the Biddles' Locust Valley days
that Newt hadn't sold off.

They sat in the Adirondack chairs. Danny opened
the beers, then carefully extracted two wet barrio
bombers from the bag. They began to eat.

"I hear you folks are planning to move up north,"
Danny said, chewing.

"Oh, yuck, has he been talking about that stupid
farm of his again?"

"I thought you were part of it."

"Part of *what*?" She chased down a spicy bite with
a mouthful of cold beer.

"It's not going to happen?"

"I honestly don't know what's going to happen, Daniel. All I know is he's been acting very hyper and
weird lately. Running around a lot. Going in and out.
And some very strange dudes have been coming by."

"Strange how?"

"Scary," she replied. "He's changed. He won't let
anyone else hang out back here anymore. He keeps
totally to himself."

"He's never been exactly what you'd call warm,"
Danny pointed out.

"He's worse. He won't even talk to *me* anymore. I
don't know what I can do. You're still the best friend
he has. He always talked to you about things. Maybe
you could . . ."

Footsteps approached from outside. The garage door
slid open and Newt strode in, toting a large suitcase.

"Greetings, Daniel. Saw your car out front. A pleasant surprise." He spotted Jenny sitting there. His nostrils flared. "Get out," he ordered her.

Jenny said, "We were just having a—"

"Get out!" he snapped.

"Don't be such an asshole!" she snapped back.

"Fuck you!"

"Fuck *you*!"

"Hey, come on," Danny broke in. "What's the big—?"

"You may go, too, Daniel, if you so desire," said Newt.

"No, no. I'll go," said Jenny, shooting a glance at Danny. "Thank you for the grub, Daniel. Good to see you again."

"Likewise."

She glowered at Newt as she left. He seemed to not notice or care. He simply slid the door closed behind her, then crossed the garage and scampered up the ladder into the rafters.

"So I brought you a bomber," Danny called up to him, "if you're still man enough to choke one down."

"Awful damned decent of you, Daniel. No time, I'm afraid. Bring me up that suitcase, would you?"

Danny hefted it. It was light. Familiar, too. "Isn't this the same suitcase we used when we stole the tape recorder?"

"Very possibly. They built them to last in those days."

Danny climbed up the ladder into the rafters. It was noticeably warmer up there. Carefully he stepped over to where Newt was crouched. Newt was pulling back a sheet that covered two eighty-pound bales of peat moss. Peat moss that wasn't peat moss.

Danny gaped at the sight of so much marijuana in one place. Its loamy smell was overpowering. "Jesus . . ."

"Please open the suitcase, Daniel."

Inside it was a scale, a roll of heavy twine, and the

Times classifieds. Newt took a sheet of the newspaper, heaped it with several handfuls of dope, and weighed it. He added some more.

"What's on your mind?" Newt asked as he worked.

"My mind?"

"Yes. You usually opt for machaca burritos when you're confronting a serious personal dilemma, as I recall."

"Grease helps me think better. Something to do with my body chemistry." Danny crouched next to him. "I've been approached about doing something and I honestly can't tell which choice is in line with my ideals. There's no clear-cut answer. No frame of reference. That, I'm discovering, is pretty much what business is all about."

Newt wrapped the dope tightly in the newspaper and tied it up with twine. He placed the bundle in the suitcase, then quickly tied up another. "I'll let you have some orange sunshine. The path will open right up, straight and true."

Danny shook his head. "Now wouldn't be a good time."

"Then look farther on down the road than you are. What truly matters, in my humble opinion, is one's vision. Anything or anyone that gets in the way of that vision must come second."

"That's easy to say. Hard to do—if somebody might get hurt."

"There are two kinds of people in this world, Daniel. People who are in charge of their lives and people who aren't. Those who are in charge of their lives end up running the lives of the others as well. The strong must carry the weak. If you're asking for my advice, it's this: concentrate on your vision. The others, they'll be no worse off than they are now. Besides, they've relinquished their right to object."

"I understand what you're saying. Only, the person

who might get hurt here is a person who is in charge of his life."

"Hmm. I see."

"What happens when two people like that clash?"

"One must lose. A simple equation. Inevitable."

"Inevitable," Danny repeated quietly.

Newt deposited a fourth bundle in the suitcase, closed it, and covered the bales back up with the sheet. "Sorry I can't stick around. Deliveries to make." He started down the ladder. "You're welcome to join me, of course."

Danny followed him down. "Uh . . ."

"Wise choice."

Jenny had gone back to work on her bike. Danny patted her on the head and waved as he and Newt passed her. Out front Newt tossed the suitcase in Queenie's side door and climbed in behind the wheel.

"So how are you?" Danny asked him through the open window.

Newt put on a pair of aviator sunglasses. "Compared to what?"

"Jenny seems to be a little worried about you. You in trouble?"

Newt snorted, which was what he did instead of laughing. Then he started up the bus. "Not as long as I keep moving, Daniel."

Danny relaxed as soon as he saw what Wendy wore: a bulky knit top, jeans, and moccasins. No see-through peignoir. No high-heeled mules. No soft music. No pass.

She grilled swordfish over the barbecue in a chrome fish holder she and Mouse got for a wedding present. It was quite tasty, and there was lots of it. They ate at the glass dining table and drank white wine. It was quiet in Mouse and Wendy's house. It felt like it was a million miles from anywhere. Sort of gave

Danny the creeps, but the evening was reasonably pleasant. Until Wendy popped the question:

"Is Michael seeing someone else?"

Actually Danny thought he handled it very maturely.
He didn't spritz her, as he had Mandy West, girl sky-
diver. He calmly and cooly put his fork down on his
plate and started to choke.

"Raise your arms!" cried Wendy, alarmed by his gag-
ging. She rushed around the table, clapped him on
the back hard. "Breathe in! *In!* You okay, Wuggy?"

He began to cough. "Have any . . . any Coke?" he
gasped.

She nodded, started for the kitchen. "Is another brand
okay?"

"Pepsi?" he managed to get out.

"No."

"RC?"

"No."

"Shasta?"

"Maybe."

"Shasta's fine. Actually, it d-doesn't matter. They
all taste the same."

She dashed through the swinging door into the
kitchen.

"As long as it isn't *diet* cola," he called.

She came back through the swinging door. "It is."

"Forget it then. I'll just have some more wine." He
took a gulp of wine. "Yeah. I'm better now. Thanks."

He poured them both some more.

She sat back down. "Is he, Wuggy?"

"What makes you say something crazy like that?"

"He's changed. He's . . . sweet. Charming. Considerate."

"Maybe he's just adjusting to married life. You
know, getting used to considering your wants and
needs. Did you think of that?"

"Yes, and I discarded it in about three and a half seconds. I think he's seeing someone."

"Say he is. I'm not, but say he is. I thought that was supposed to be okay. You know, your experiment."

"It is," she agreed readily. "In theory. Only, I've made a very unpleasant discovery about myself. I am by nature a jealous person."

"You're just finding that out?"

"Mostly I went out with you. You never gave me a reason to be jealous. Or sorry." She sat back and puffed out her cheeks. "It's just not working, Danny," she said wearily.

"The experiment?"

"The marriage."

"Wendy, it's only been a *month*. It takes time for two people to get used to each other. It's something you have to work at. I mean, we're talking about a life-long commitment here, not a Big Mac with fries. You guys, you should really talk."

"He's always at the agency, or on the phone, or . . . About this trip to Vegas of his . . ."

Danny shifted in his chair. It was made of white wicker and managed to be both not nice to look at and not comfortable. "What about it?"

"Does he have someone with him?"

"I wouldn't know."

"You would, too. He respects you, and he wants you to respect him."

"He does?"

"He does. He thinks you're idealistic but not a hyp-ocrite like the others."

Danny tugged at his ear. "Yeah, well, it's pretty easy to be idealistic when you aren't getting other choices foisted on you. Then it gets hard. Especially when it's just you."

"It doesn't have to be just you."

"It doesn't?"

"Danny, what if I told you that I'm seriously con-sidering asking Michael for a divorce. How would you feel about that? Could we start seeing each other again? Would it be okay?"

"Wendy, you made a commitment. It's supposed to mean something."

"All it means is I'm not happy. I've never been so totally miserable in my whole life. How can that be a positive thing? Tell me."

Danny didn't have an answer. He wanted to go home.

"It's Rachel, isn't it," she said quietly.

"What's Rachel got to do with it?" he asked.

"I happen to know something," she advised him, raising an eyebrow.

Danny leaned forward. "What?"

"First you have to admit it."

"*Tell* me."

"*Admit* it. You love her."

"Well, I don't know if I'd go that—"

"You *love* her."

"Okay," he conceded gravely. "I l-love her."

"I knew it."

"Now tell me what you know."

"She feels the same way about you."

Danny's pulse quickened. "She does?"

"Uh-huh."

"Did she say something?"

"No."

"Then how do you—?"

"I know."

"*How?*"

"I'm her best friend. I know the signs. The way she acts around you. Looks at you." Wendy stuck out her lower lip, drew it back in. "You know, it's totally amazing. She *always* gets what she wants. And to think I had you all those years and I let you get away." She shook her head. "I've really blown it."

"*I love you, Rachel . . .*"

Danny was on the forklift, moving skids of Oriental-
style cement lanterns suitable for planting or target
practice. It was strictly a mechanical job: Go to pile.
Lower fork. Lift fork. Deliver. Approach. Lower
fork. Wait for Freddy and Tommy to unload. Return
to pile. That was fine with Danny. It left his mind
free to work on his speech:

"I love you, Rachel . . ."

No beating around the bush. Just the three magic
words. Okay, four words.

"I love you, Rachel . . ."

Or was it better the other way around?

"Rachel, I love you . . ."

No. Too melodramatic. Better the way he had it
first. More natural. More him. He would say it today, as soon as he got home. Why wait? She believed
what he believed. She had a conscience. Taste. She
felt the same way about him. He loved her. Always
had. Always would. She may as well know it now.
Before they got old and died.

"I love you, Rachel . . ."

"Me too, Danny."

"Yo, Porky!" called Freddy as he hefted the last of
the lantern crates.

Danny raised an inquiring eyebrow.

Freddy and Tommy both flashed him their stoner
grins. Time to visit the john.

"Me too, Danny."

They were waiting for him in stall number one, cigarettes going. Freddy lit the joint. It was a bomber
the approximate length and diameter of the bat Frank
Howard used when he batted cleanup for the Dodgers. New dope, Tommy pointed out. They smoked
the entire thing. Danny knew this was a major mistake as soon as he reeled back out onto the warehouse
floor.

His body parts were flying off in many different
directions.

His head . . . his head was way up there in the rafters. He ordered it back down where it belonged, only
it bounced right back up there again. He felt just like
a bobble doll, with springs for limbs. Boing. Boing.
Boiiiiiinggg. Oops. There went his arms. *Boiiiiiinggg.*
Legs, too. *Boiiiiiinggg.* Make way for . . . Bobbleman.
B-b-bobble. B-b-bobble.

No problem getting back up onto the forklift. Just
j-j-jump. T-t-ta-da. He started her up. Looked both
ways. *Boiiiiiinggg.* Proceeded to the pile, lowered the
fork, completely missed the skid he was aiming at.
Wasn't close enough. The dope was messing with his
depth perception. B-b-bobble. He inched forward.
Got it.

"Me too, Danny."

What if she *did* say that? Then what?

He checked behind him, pulled away from the pile,
and cruised across the warehouse floor to the truck
bed, careful not to stop too far away this time.

Tommy waved at him. "Back her up, dude!" he
yelled. "You're too close!"

Danny nodded. *Boiiiiiinggg.* Threw her in reverse.
Pulled back.

"Hold it!" Freddy yelled.

They began to unload.

"Me too, Danny."

That meant marriage. Staying put. No way out.
Ever.

"Am I wrong?"

Fear. Heart-pounding fear. Hot. Sweaty. *Fear.*

"Am I wrong?"

Tommy was waving at him again and pointing. He
wanted Danny to move up a touch. So he did. Only
the forklift didn't move forward. It moved backward.
He was still in reverse. He tried to reach for the gear
shifter. He really did. But his b-b-bobble arm just didn't
want to cooperate. And he was going faster now.
Faster than he could handle.

He was out of control.

Workers were diving out of his way, yelling.

Stop it. He had to stop it. Real bright idea, except for one small detail—he couldn't remember how to stop it!

There was Abe. Gee, what was Abe doing there? He was talking on the phone. And now he was looking up, and his jaw was dropping, and . . . *ka-smashhh* . . . Danny's vision of him exploded and then it was clear again and Abe was diving out of the way and Danny smashed hard into something that didn't give way. Abe's big desk. The forklift stopped dead. Danny didn't. He flew through the air, landed spread-eagled on Abe's credenza. Landed on his own bar mitzvah pictures, dazed.

Abe shut off the forklift. Glass crunched underfoot. Bobby was there now, standing where the glass wall to Abe's office had been. And Pip. And Irv and Larry. All of them were staring at him, eyes wide with horror.

Abe kneeled next to him. Sniffed at his breath. Peered into his eyes. "You okay, kiddo?"

Danny nodded.

"Remember you said you wanted to be treated like an adult?"

Danny nodded.

"Remember you said you wanted to be treated like any other employee?"

Danny nodded.

"Kiddo, you're fired."

"I love you, Rachel . . ."

Actually, it was better this way. Pier West was out of his life for good now. He could start fresh. A new life. Their life. The two of them together.

It was a little past noon when Danny pulled up in front of the shack. Her VW was in the driveway. He grabbed the flowers he'd bought on Lincoln Boulevard, took a deep breath, and headed inside, step sure, head clear. Well, clearer than two hours before.

It was very quiet in the house. He could hear the kitchen faucet dripping.

"Rooms?" he called out.

She wasn't in the living room.

"Rooms?"

She wasn't in the kitchen.

"Rooms?"

"I love you, Rachel . . ."

Her bedroom door was half open. She was still in bed, the little lazybones.

He took another deep breath. Then he pushed the door open and plunged inside her room with his flowers and said it.

Danny said, "I love you, Rachel."

He said it loud and clear and firm. And then he was ready for anything.

Except Rachel's reaction.

She just stared at him with her mouth open. She was utterly and completely mortified.

Rachel wasn't alone in the bed.

Chapter Twelve

The road wasn't as much fun as the big fella remembered.

It took him three hours to get his first ride north. Three whole hours standing there in the hot sun on Pacific Coast Highway with his thumb out. Drivers ignored him. Little kids made faces at him in the back window. And when he finally did get a ride—from a surfer with a van—he only got as far as the signals that stopped Highway 101 in downtown Santa Barbara.

There he now stood, crowded onto the shoulder with dozens of freaks holding signs. Signs for Berkeley. Signs for Alaska. Signs for Anywhere.

He was slightly sorry he'd left his MG at Abe and Ev's. But he wanted no things, just as he wanted no attachments, no responsibilities. He had only his clothes, his Swiss Army knife, and thirty-six dollars. Inside the small knapsack he'd bought were a mess kit, a canteen, a cup, and a rough wool blanket. Plenty.

It felt good to be alone again. Alone was the best way to be.

Craig. That was his name. He had a 29-inch waist and shoulders out to here and long blond hair. He was the kind of guy who was totally at ease no matter

how embarrassing the circumstances. He had met
"Rache" at the beach. A very funny story, really. See,
his Trans Am had bumped her Vee-dub in the lot
and they got to rapping and . . . Danny handled it very
maturely. He did. He shook Craig's hand. Then he
apologized for barging in and mumbled something
about having to go fertilize the lawn.

Rachel never stopped staring at him with her mouth
open.

He really should murder Wendy.

What an oaf he was. The biggest oaf in the world.
You are who you are. He was an oaf. O-A-F.

And he was stranded in Santa Barbara. He had almost given up hope when a trucker picked him up
around dinner time and took him another twenty-five
miles north, as far as the Gaviota truck stop. There
he bought a few necessities—bread, butter, Baby Ruths,
instant coffee, a toothbrush, more Baby Ruths.

Across the highway there was a rocky, deserted little beach and a dozen campsites tucked into a gap at
the base of the shoreline cliffs. A metal railroad bridge
spanned directly overhead, joining the cliffs together.
The Gaviota Trestle. He had been told once that it was
a fine place to catch a nighttime freighter.

The tide was going out, uncovering the big rocks at
the base of the cliffs. Abalones were fixed to them.
Danny opened his Swiss Army knife and pried one
loose. Upside down it looked like a big fat tongue
lolling around inside a helmet. Gross, but it didn't have
teeth or claws, and, if properly cooked, it tasted good.

Danny made a fire at one of the campsites, then
washed the abalone under the tap, cut it out of its
shell, and sliced it into quarter-inch steaks. When the
fire was hot he laid his little mess kit skillet on the
grill over it, peeled some of his butter into it, and fried
the steaks until they were golden brown. He devoured them with slices of bread. Still hungry, he fried
some more. When all the steaks were gone he boiled

some water and drank black coffee with one of his Baby Ruths. He watched the fire burn down.

This was a good life. Orderly. Self-sufficient. Better. He'd go as far as Salinas. Pick whatever was being picked now. Then go farther north. Hook on with a tuna boat again. It made sense this way. Meal to meal. Season to season. It made a lot of sense.

There was barbed wire at the trestle supports to keep people from climbing up the cliff and out onto the tracks. It had been cut. Danny wriggled through and started climbing. A few trees clung to the side of the hill near the bottom. Then it got very steep and rocky, with crumbly topsoil. He had to scamper up fast to make it, but he did, taking the skin off one palm and one knee. There was a slope of gravel and then he was up, panting, on the tracks.

There was the odor of raw seaweed up there. The salty breeze zinged at his nostrils. It wasn't completely dark yet. He could still make out the Channel Islands in the distance. Behind him were the golden foothills.

The trestle was wide enough for one set of tracks. Danny parked his ample flanks on the rail and waited. For luck he laid some pennies out on the rail. It darkened. There was a quarter moon, and stars.

The northbound signal light was the first one to turn again. Danny scampered across the trestle and lay on his belly in the gravel bed next to an old deserted railroad shack.

First there was a glow from the south. Brighter. Brighter still. Then it was an engine noise. A hum. Then the glow began to form into a beam. The hum became a roar. And then the train was coming around the bend and heading right for him, its headlight big and bright as the kliegs that lit up Hollywood Boulevard movie premieres when Danny was little. Danny tensed, readied himself to hop aboard when it slowed. For a second the train seemed frozen in the night.

Hardly looked like it was moving at all. But it was. It was roaring. Bearing down on him. It wasn't slowing down. Its giant beam lit up the trestle and made everything around him into daylight. The ground shook, the rails sang. Danny shut his eyes tight, covered his ears, and pressed flat against the grade.

KAPOWWWWWWWWWWWWWWWW . . .

It tore past him, shaking him, pelting him with gravel and grit. One car and another and another. He pressed even tighter against the ground. And another and . . .

. . . *KAPOWWWWWWWWWWWWWWW*

It was by him, its tail lights receding into the darkness. Silence.

Danny started breathing again. He got to his feet and felt a rail. It was hot. By the moonlight he found a few of his flattened pennies and pocketed them. Then he sighed and sat back down on the rail. Sure wasn't his idea of a fine place to catch a freighter.

It had been a long day. He was thinking about climbing back down and curling up at a campsite for the night when he saw another green signal light from the south. *And* one from the north. Ah, this was it. Sure—the trestle had only one track.

He went back to his perch and watched as the glows got brighter from both directions. Watched as the northbound freighter slowed and came to a halt on the switching tracks just before the trestle. There it waited, huge engine heaving, as the southbound train made its way across the trestle.

Danny crept alongside it until he found an open freight car. He poked his head inside. It was empty. He planted both hands firmly and hoisted himself up. The top half of his body made it. The bottom half didn't. His legs paddled around helplessly in midair. Danny cursed, dropped back down, tore off his knapsack and tossed it in. Just needed more freedom of movement. Sure, that's what it was. With a one, two, three *hut* he gave it another shot. Got most of his body in this time, and one leg. And it was a good thing, too, because the train was starting to move again. He strained and strained until he made it all the way in, gasping for air.

He was on his way.

Chapter Thirteen

The first thing Danny did was grope around in the dark freight car until he found his knapsack. The train was making its way across the trestle now and picking up speed. It was moving fast by the time it reached the cliff on the other side.

The second thing he did was jump off.

He landed in the sloped gravel bed on his best padded side, slid a few yards down, and came to a stop in some brush. The lights of the train disappeared around the bend. Slowly he made his way back down the hill. Then he found his campsite, curled up in his blanket with his knapsack under his head, and looked up at the stars.

He couldn't go away. He couldn't run just because things hadn't turned out the way he wanted. A man didn't do that. Not a man who believed in stuff. Not a man who was respected by other people. *Loved.* He stayed. He fought. That's what a man did. At least that was Danny's personal philosophy. Danny wasn't going anywhere, except back.

He slept. When morning came he groaned from the stiffness in his limbs and got slowly to his feet. He was getting too old to sleep on the ground. His eyes felt gritty, his face stubbly and itchy. His stomach growled.

The highway was deserted. It was still very early. Danny crossed the road and put away buckwheat cakes, sausages, and hot coffee at the truck stop counter. He considered calling Irv from the pay phone to tell him he had decided to sell his fifty percent of Pier West. He had no other choice. Abe wasn't going to change with the times—at least not quick enough for it to matter. He had to be forced. This was the only way. It was the best thing for Pier West. Pier West was what mattered. Abe would have reached the same decision himself—back in the days when he wasn't so afraid. Danny fished a dime out of his jeans, then realized Irv was probably still home in bed. He'd call him when he got to L.A.

The trucker on the stool next to Danny was making a morning run to Tarzana. Danny paid for his breakfast in exchange for a lift.

He got dropped about a mile from Mouse and Wendy's and set off on foot, hoping Mouse hadn't left for work yet. He'd be able to give him a lift over the hill.

Mouse was eating a bagel when he opened the door. He wore a black silk dressing gown that had his initials stitched in white on his left breast. His eyes widened when he saw Danny.

"Jesus, Levine, where the hell you been? I've been looking all over town for you!"

"You have? What for?"

"Your mom asked me to." Mouse ushered him inside, put a hand on Danny's shoulder. "It's your old man, boychick. He's had another heart attack."

"What do you mean *another* heart attack?"

"He had one your senior year of high school," Ev replied calmly, as the two of them stood in the cor-

ridor outside Abe's intensive care room at Mt. Sinai
Hospital on Beverly Boulevard. "When you were
away camping over Christmas."

"Why didn't anybody ever say anything?!"

"It was a small one, and he didn't want anyone to
know."

"I'm his *son!*"

"He's been fine. He takes his medication."

"I haven't seen him take a single pill my whole life."

"He hid them from you."

Danny shook his head. "I don't get it, Mom."

"He didn't want you coming to work for the wrong
reason. He wanted you to feel you had a choice."

"He is so ridiculous."

"He's not perfect, sweetheart. Believe me, I know."

"Will he be okay?"

"This one was bigger. But Dr. Newman thinks so,
provided he cuts back on his workload."

"No way. He'll never do it."

"We've got to get him to."

"Mom, it's a one-man show. Who's going to. . . ?"
Danny stopped short, struck by a bolt of total, over-
whelming terror. He took several breaths.

"Are you all right, sweetheart?"

Danny swallowed. It passed. He nodded. "Can I see
him?"

Abe was propped up in bed, working on a cross-
word puzzle, his glasses pushed down to the tip of
his nose, which had a tube up it. Bandages were stuck
all over the insides of his forearms. He looked weak
and tired.

He didn't sound it though. "Where the hell you
been?"

"Calm, Abe," Ev pleaded. "Calm."

"I took a trip," Danny replied. "That okay?"

"Sure. What do I care where you go? What the hell
happened to your face?"

Danny scratched his chin. "Didn't shave for a couple days."

"You look like a jerk," Abe said to him. Then to Ev he said, "I can't look at him. I'm getting upset. I'm not supposed to get upset. Ev, do me a favor and get him my razor. In my kit there."

"No, no. I'm fine," Danny assured her. "So how are you feeling, Pop?"

"He can shave in the sink right there. Get him the lather, too, Ev. The Noxzema."

"That's okay, Mom. Later. So how are you feeling, Pop?"

"And a towel, Ev. He'll need a—"

"Stop this!" ordered Danny. "I want to know how you are and I want to know this minute!"

"Ah, I'm okay. Back on my feet in—"

"Dr. Newman said no work for at least one month this time," Ev said. "Walk a mile every morning after breakfast. And *relax*."

"Fooey. I got a business to run."

"You're going to have to let up, Pop."

"Don't tell me what to do," Abe snapped.

"I'd better go," Danny said to Ev. "He obviously doesn't want me here."

"He's still upset about what happened with the forklift," she said.

"It was an accident," Danny told her.

"He said you acted like a child."

"What did you say?"

"I said if you treat someone like a child they respond like one."

"And what did he say?"

"He said if—"

"Would you two stop talking about me like I'm dead!" cried Abe.

"Who from the office knows about this?" Danny asked him.

"Nobody. They find out you sprung a leak in your chest and the wolves are all over you."

"What wolves?"

"Import Barn. And they got U-Buy money behind 'em now."

Danny leaned forward. "Oh yeah? Since when?"

"Since Friday. They got bought out."

"No kidding?"

"Top secret. Under wraps for a couple more weeks. I got a source over there. I also got big competition now, like I don't need."

"Dad phoned in and said he was taking a business trip to San Francisco," Ev said. "He's been checking in by phone every few hours."

"That won't work for more than a day or two, Pop. We'll have to do something."

"Who's *we*?" demanded Abe. "Last I heard you was a warehouseman. And a crappy one at that."

"Look, Pop. I know we had a disagreement. I'm prepared to put it behind us if you are. The company comes first."

"Your father's health comes first," said Ev.

"What do you care about the company?" Abe asked him sharply.

"I care, okay?" replied Danny, equally sharply.

"Calm, Abe," Ev commanded.

"Ev, we got business to discuss, will ya? Leave us alone for five minutes."

"You're supposed to be resting," she pointed out.

"I'll be right out, Mom," Danny promised.

"Okay," she said, reluctantly. "But don't get him upset."

He led her out, closed the door behind her. Abe glared at him. He glared at Abe. Another stalemate.

Danny got a glass of water and took a drink. "You want me back?" he finally said.

Abe crossed his arms, didn't answer him.

"You fired me. You have to say you want me back."

Abe just stuck his chin out.

Danny stood at the window, looked down at the cars passing on Beverly. "I get it. You're not going to admit you need me or my help. That would be a sign of weakness. So it's up to me to . . . volunteer to do what I can. Until you get back on your feet. How's that?"

"And then what?"

"That's up to you."

"Fair enough." Abe shifted uneasily in the bed. "Okay. It's up to me to . . . to say I can't handle it myself right now. I need ya to run things for me until I get back."

"And then what?"

"That's up to you."

"When you say run things do you mean—?"

"Run things."

"You mean—?"

"Run things," Abe repeated.

"Shouldn't you bring in an experienced top administrator? A grownup?"

"What for?"

Danny sat down. "You'll have to guide me. I won't know how you'd handle certain things."

"No."

Danny frowned. "No?"

"If you're gonna run the company, you're gonna run it your way. If you try to guess what I'd do, you'll be lost. You got to be yourself. I'll help you, but you gotta be you."

Danny moved his chair closer to the head of Abe's bed. "Pop . . . ?"

Abe softened. "Yo, kiddo?"

"You were right, when you fired me. I didn't respond like a man. I-I'm sorry."

"You got a lot to offer, kiddo. I wish there was time for you to come along slow, but I need you now. You're up to it. You know how things work. You know right

from wrong. Officially, I'll be away on a trip for a
month. Unofficially, I'll be right here next to the
phone. You got me any time you need me. Mom,
too."

"Pip?"

"Pip, sure. And my Turks. You can trust them.
They can know what really happened to me. Just them.
Nobody else."

Irv and Larry would both be pleased by this. An orderly, natural changing of the guard. No buyout
necessary.

"Okay, Pop."

"When I come back, it'll be as chairman of the
board."

"There's going to be a board?"

"You wanted one—it's your baby now. You'll be
the president. Personally, if it was me, I'd hold on
to veto power . . ."

"We'll talk about it."

"Sure, sure. That we got time for. We'll draw up
papers. Make an announcement. This is it, kiddo.
Your time has come. Sooner than I expected, but some
things you can't control. What do ya say?"

Danny took a deep breath, let it out slowly. "You
know what I'm going to say."

"I wanna hear you say it, D.L."

"I say . . . okay, A.L."

Danny stuck out his hand. Abe stuck out his own,
which wavered there in the air a little. They shook
on it.

And then something totally amazing happened to
Abe. He became an old man right before Danny's
eyes. The lines in his face deepened. His posture slumped.
He *shrank*. Danny found himself staring at him, stunned.
And found Abe staring right back at him, equally
stunned.

"What is it, Pop?"

"Must be the dope they gave me." Even his voice

sounded feeble now. "You look . . . *different* to me
all of a sudden."

"Different how?"

Abe didn't answer.

Danny went over to the mirror above the sink. He
needed a shave. Otherwise he looked the same as
always.

He turned to tell Abe this, only Abe was snoring
softly now. Quietly, so as not to wake him, Danny
got the lather and razor out of his kit, turned on the
hot water tap, and began to shave.

Mouse's agency was near the hospital. Danny met
him for a drink on a stretch of La Cienega that had
been called Restaurant Row when he was a kid. Ol-
lie Hammond's had been here. Stear's for Steaks. Richlor's.
The Mediterranean. A whole row of fancy restaurants
where fancy people like Dean Martin and Efrem Zim-
balist, Jr. ate. Now there was Alan Hale's Lobster Bar-
rel. As they went inside, Alan Hale, Jr., the burly,
white-haired actor who played the Skipper on *Gilligan's
Island,* greeted them at the door with a grin and a
hearty handshake. "Ahoy, little buddies!" he boomed
out. "Welcome to my restaurant!"

They sat at the bar. Danny ordered a beer, Mouse a
tequila sunrise.

"Some day, huh?" said Mouse glumly.

"I'll say. I just got some pretty strange news from
my—"

"I find this young comic at one of the improv clubs,
see? Fifty cents a night he's making. I get Annie hot
for him. We take him on. Get him the second lead in
a new fall sitcom. This morning he decides he wants
to pull out. They've already taped the first three shows.
All day I'm holding his hand. Meanwhile, I gotta
spend one solid hour on the phone with Wendy. What
does she want from me, Levine?"

"She's your wife."

"Yeah, but lately she keeps wanting to *communicate,* share her *feelings* with me. I don't know what got her started on this. She's making me crazy. Know what she says to me today? 'A marriage, Mickey, isn't a Whopper with cheese.' "

"Big Mac with fries."

"I've had it, Levine. I'm gonna ask her for a divorce. Let her make some other guy miserable. Mandy's more my style. Quiet. Obedient. We have great sex together. Wild sex. Wendy and me, we got zilch in common. I believe in admitting when something's a bust. Making a clean break. Otherwise it could drag on for—"

"Weeks."

"What do you think? Am I at fault here?"

"I do think you're being a little inconsiderate, Stern."

"You do? How?"

"You're only thinking about yourself."

"I should think more about her?"

"You should think more about other people, period."

"See, that's what I love about you, Levine. You understand 'people' things. Gimme a for instance, okay?"

"Okay. Take me, as a for instance. I've just come from the intensive care ward of the hospital. My father, who has a tube up his nose, has decided I should take over the entire business. Meanwhile, yesterday I happened to find the only woman I've ever loved in bed with someone named Craig. My life is in a state of utter chaos—possibly even ruin—and you haven't so much as asked me how I'm doing! You don't care! All you're interested in is your job and your girlfriend's pussy!"

"Okay, okay. Cool down. I read ya, Levine."

"I'm perfectly cool. You asked me for a for instance. I gave you one."

Mouse ordered them another round. "How *is* your old man?"

"He wants me to take over—that's how he is."

"Pay hike?"

"We didn't get into that." Danny ran his hands through his hair. "There's no way I can handle it, Stern. No way."

"You can do it, Levine," Mouse assured him. "It's inside you. The tools. The breeding. All you need is the experience. And nobody's got that until they got it."

"I'm not ready."

"No one's ever ready. It gets thrust on you. Like a mugging. Like Harry Truman. Like love."

"There is no such thing as love," said Danny. "You were right about that."

"No offense, but hard-boiled you don't pull off so good. I meant to talk to you about Snooks."

"Nothing to talk about."

"So why'd you bring it up?"

"As a for instance." Danny sipped his beer. "I made a total oaf of myself, Stern. Presumed."

"Presumed what?"

"That something could ever happen between us." Danny sighed. "And to think I actually buried a rodent for that woman."

"You didn't make an oaf out of yourself, Levine. She did."

"*She* did?"

'You ought to talk to her. You ought to make an effort to *communicate*."

"I may have to make an effort to sit on you."

Mouse cackled. "Talk to her."

"What's the point?"

"As a favor, okay?"

"She does still have all my clothes. I mean, I have to go get 'em anyway."

"Atta boy." Mouse drained his drink. "Seriously, Levine. You think I shouldn't dump Wendy?"

"I told you I wasn't perfect."

Danny hadn't heard her come in the house. He stopped folding the clothes he'd laid out on his mat and glanced up at her. She stood in the bedroom doorway wearing jeans, a T-shirt, and an apprehensive expression. She looked lovely.

He went back to his folding. "I know you did," he said quietly.

"What are you doing?"

"Thought I ought to be at home with my mom for a while. My pop's in—"

"The hospital, I know. How is he?"

"Nuts." Danny stowed his socks in his duffel bag.

"Is that the only reason you're moving out?" she asked.

"Dunno."

"Why are you having so much trouble looking at me?"

"I'm not."

"You are. You can't look me in the eye."

"I'm embarrassed, okay?" he blurted out.

"Because you said you love me?"

Danny shrugged, reddening.

"Danny, the last thing I wanted to do was hurt you. But I had to do what I did."

He gathered up his shoes.

"Look at me, damn it!"

He looked at her. She had tears in her eyes.

"I had to find out if it would mean anything to sleep with some gorgeous hunk. Some guy who doesn't know me. Doesn't care. Some guy who means shit to me. I was testing myself on another Ricky. You just happened to walk in on it. It was bad timing."

"When you're a guy like me," Danny said, "it's always bad timing."

"Stop it, will you? I'm trying to explain: I didn't feel anything. I was too busy holding myself in, protecting myself. It wasn't any good. Don't you know why?"

He shook his head.

"Because I've finally seen what love is. It's a very dear, very old friend who's the one person in the world I can confide in, and trust and be myself around. The one person who knows me and still cares about me. The one person who makes me happy."

Danny swallowed. "Would that . . . would this person happen to have a slight weight problem?"

She smiled. "Very slight."

"Gee . . ."

"That's all you have to say? 'Gee'?"

Danny hitched up his jeans, crossed the room, and boldly took Rachel Stern in his arms. Her body melted into his.

"Gee . . ." he said.

"Gee . . ." she said.

The phone rang just as they were about to kiss. She cursed under her breath, went and answered it in her room.

"It's your father!" she called to him.

"Kiddo, we got a lot to talk over," Abe said when Danny took the phone from Rachel. "For starters, we gotta roll on American Heritage if we want to stay in the lead."

Rachel patted the bed next to her. Danny sat.

"How soon can you get over here?" Abe asked.

Danny covered the receiver. "He wants to know how soon I can get over there."

She touched his face, ran her tongue around the edge of his ear. "Tell him tomorrow," she whispered. "Not too early."

"Tomorrow, not too early," Danny repeated into the phone, his voice quavering a little.

Rachel began to unbutton Danny's shirt.

"But kiddo—"

"Get some sleep, Pop. That's an order."

Rachel finished unbuttoning Danny's shirt and pulled it off him.

"I don't like this new arrangement at all," grumbled Abe.

Rachel began to unbuckle Danny's belt.

"That's f-funny, Pop. I sure do."

Later as she cuddled against him under the single sheet, her hair loose and silken on his chest, Danny broke into song:

> *A horse is a horse*
> *Of course, of course.*
> *And no one can talk to a horse*
> *Of course.*
> *That is, of course,*
> *Unless the horse*
> *Is the famous Mister Ed.*

When this failed to get the slightest reaction out of her he launched into verse two:

> *Go right to the source*
> *And ask the horse*

"Enough!" she cried, laughing.

"Remember it now?"

"Every word of it."

"Care to sing along?"

"Do I have a choice?"

"No."

Together they sang:

> *Go right to the source*
> *And ask the horse*
> *He'll give you the answer*
> *That you'll endorse.*
> *He's always on a steady course*
> *Talk to Mister Ed.*

They sang the whole theme song at the top of their lungs in Rachel's bed.

And then Danny said, "I just realized something. You know that fear of mine? I don't have anything to be afraid of, at least not as far as you and me goes. What other couple in history has ever been able to say that the 'Mister Ed' theme song is 'our' song?"

"Is it?"

"Of course."

She laughed. She laughed very easily now. Possibly it was that third orgasm.

"I mean, fifty years from now people will ask us what 'our' song is and we'll tell them and they'll know we're different. Always were. Even our grandchildren will know."

She stiffened. "Our . . . grandchildren?"

"Oops. Am I blowing it?"

She didn't answer for a while. "No," she finally said. "No, you're not. It's just happening a little fast."

"Not for me it isn't."

"No?"

"See, we've been married for a long, long time, you and me. You just didn't know about it."

"How'd you get to be so sweet?"

"How'd you get to be so cute?"

"It's a full time job, believe me."

"I don't."

"Men are so easily fooled," she said. "That's the best thing about you."

"The best?"

She buried her face in his chest and purred contentedly. "One of the best."

"You sure do smell good."

"It's just Bluegrass toilet water. Same as always."

"Yeah, that's what I thought . . ."

"Will you still like me if I'm a lawyer?"

"You're going to be a lawyer?"

"I applied for late enrollment to UCLA this morning. I think I should get in."

"You won't lose any of your cuteness will you?"

"I don't think so."

"Then it's okay. Will you still like me if I'm p-president of Pier West?"

"Promise not to change?"

"I have no intention of changing."

"Promise?"

"Uh-huh."

"Then I'll still like you." She raised herself up on her elbows. Her face was right over his now. "Danny?" she said very softly.

"Yeah?"

"Was I worth the wait?"

"Uh-huh. You were . . ."

"I was what?"

"You were perfect."

Chapter Fourteen

There were no cars in the Pier West parking lot yet.
Lesson number four—the boss always gets in first.

The boss unlocked the front door and flicked on the
lights in the reception area. Then he straightened his
tie, thrust back his shoulders, and strode command-
ingly down the corridor, waving and calling hearty
good mornings to his invisible front office staff. Not
satisfied, he went back to the reception area and tried
it again, concentrating more on warmth and vitality.
Better. Friendlier. More him.

He would have felt a lot more in command if his
forehead hadn't decided to break out.

The glass wall in Abe's office had been repaired. The
warehouse floor was dark on the other side. Danny
took off his jacket, rolled up his sleeves, and went to
work taking down all the photos of himself that
adorned the credenza, the end tables, the walls.

Then he faced Abe's desk chair. It was even taller
and more imposing than Danny's had been. Danny
swivelled it, hesitated, gingerly sat. He leaned back.
Farther. All the way back. It didn't throw him.

Respect.

There was a Rolodex on Abe's desk. And trays crammed with shipping statements. And spikes with invoices stuck on them. And stacks of messages. And a paperweight Danny made for Abe when he was about seven out of a blob of clay with a clown's face painted on it. The design came from the back of the child's menu at Hodie's coffee shop, which had rubber bands on it to go around his ears. He would wear it at the table like a mask until Abe made him take it off because he said he looked like a jerk.

He put the paperweight in the top drawer of the desk.

Abe had scribbled dollar figures all over his calendar blotter. And practiced his signature, here with a great flourish, there with a hurried, spare stroke. And doodled. Doodles were supposed to reveal a lot about a person. Abe's were concentric circles.

A newspaper clipping was stuck in one corner of the blotter. An ad:

Substantial before need savings!
Now through August 30 only
10 to 25 percent off list price
on lawn and wall crypts.
Bring in this ad for additional
savings on your purchase.
Hillside Memorial Park and Mortuary
6001 Centinela Ave.

Danny stared at it a second. Then he dove for the phone.

"You know me and a sale, kiddo," Abe said when Danny finished yelling. "Don't matter what it is as long as I can get it off-price."

"Are you going to die?" demanded Danny. "You'd tell me, right? You didn't tell me about the other heart attack. For all I know, this is really your third or your fourth or—"

"Just a coincidence," Abe assured him. "My word

on it. Happened to see the ad a few weeks ago. I get twenty off it'll cover my whole mortuary fee. Figured I may as well—"

"You're not going anywhere?"

"Nope, ain't getting rid of me yet. Why, getting a little shook?"

"I'm fine. Pretty quiet here so far."

"Stands to reason—it's only a quarter to seven."

"Thought I may as well beat the traffic."

"Relax. Any questions, I'll be right here. They even bathe me here, like a little baby. Okay?"

"Okay, Pop."

Danny hung up to find Pip standing in the office doorway. He was so happy to see her he almost ran over and hugged her. She looked pretty pleased herself.

"Welcome back," she said.

"Nice to be back. You're in early."

"Thought *you'd* be. Coffee? Nate started the pot."

"Good old Natey. Please. Milk, no sugar."

"I remember."

When she came back with it she placed it before Danny on Abe's desk and sat down across from him.

"You clear it with Mr. Bell so you can be my assistant again?" Danny asked.

"All clear. Now please tell me what's going on."

Danny took a sip of his coffee. "Officially, my father and mother are on vacation in Israel for one month."

"How nice for them."

"I'm keeping an eye on things until he gets back."

Pip pursed her lips. "Unofficially?"

"Heart attack."

"Serious?"

Danny wadded up the clipping in front of him and threw it in the wastebasket. He'd made that, too, from a Baskin Robbins one-gallon ice cream container and Chanuka wrapping paper. "Serious enough. Only nobody is supposed to know. Except the Turks. I'll tell them myself as soon as they get in."

She nodded, looked around at the office. "Is this for good?"

"When he returns it'll be as chairman of the board."

"There's gonna be a—?"

"I'll be p-president."

"Congratulations. Can I still call you Danny?"

"You'd better. There'll be a lot of changes around here, Pip. They won't happen overnight, but they'll happen. We'll make them happen."

The lights came on in the warehouse. Danny could see bodies and crates moving around on the floor now. There was his old boss, Bobby Clarke.

"Anything I can do now?" Pip asked.

"Draw up a memo?"

She fetched her pad, sat.

" 'B.C.—' " dictated Danny. " 'Please have all stall doors removed from the men's rooms on the warehouse floor as soon as possible. Thank you for your cooperation. D.L.' Check that, make it Bobby and Danny. I hate initials."

"Why do you want the stall doors removed?"

"He'll understand."

"More coffee?"

"Please."

"Poison wagon's probably here now. Doughnut?"

"No, thanks."

"Cruller? Bear's claw?"

"Nope. Nope."

Her eyes widened. "Well, well."

He grinned sheepishly.

"Well, well, well. I wonder if she knows how lucky she is."

"I'm the lucky one."

"That's the trouble with this world. All the nice guys get taken."

"You're starting to sound like Schultzy on *Love that Bob*."

"I'm starting to look like her, too."

Danny laughed. "Get out of here. And get me a new wastebasket when you get a chance, please."

She nodded. Within a minute Danny could hear her typing up his memo.

He sat back. Not bad so far. Commanding. Confident. Casual. He reached into his trouser pocket, pulled out his train pennies from Gaviota, and put them in the ashtray on the desk. Then he sat all the way back in his chair, feet up, hands clasped behind his head, and watched the activity out on his floor.

"Surprise, surprise!" Danny called out from behind Abe's desk.

Irv and Larry stood there in the office doorway, clearly shocked.

"Wha . . . How?" was all Larry could manage.

Irv got his wits back first. "Hey, welcome back," he said, stepping forward with a grin and a handshake.

"Thanks. Nice to be here. Sit, sit."

They sat.

"You may be wondering what I'm doing in The Czar's office."

"Good guess," said Larry, anxiously lighting a cigarette.

"I have some rather strange news for you guys. Remember you asked me about selling my half of Pier West so the three of us could move up?"

They nodded.

"Well, due to a certain unforeseen development, that's no longer going to be—"

The buzz of his phone interrupted him.

"Excuse me," he said, reaching for it.

"You alone, kiddo?" Abe sounded agitated.

"No, you okay?"

"Get alone. *Right* now."

"Okay. Sure. Whatever you say." He covered the receiver. "Could you guys excuse me for a second? Personal call."

They stepped out. Danny closed the door after them.
"Okay, Pop, I'm alone. What's up?"

"Bad news is what's up. Just got a tip from my little voice over at Import Barn. Guess what they got
on the drawing board? *Top secret.*"

"What?"

"An American Heritage line—tied in to the bicentennial."

"Kind of a coincidence, huh?"

"It's no coincidence, kiddo."

Danny suddenly felt very warm. "It's not?"

"Hell no. One of our people tipped 'em off."

"You're kidding."

"I am not kidding. We have a low-down, two-
timing *gonif* in our midst. Who knew about American Heritage besides you and me and the Turks?"

"Nobody. Just Pip, but she wouldn't—"

"It's not Pip. This is somebody with top level con-
tacts over there. It's one of the Turks. Maybe both
of 'em."

"It can't be."

"Don't tell me it can't be! It *is!*"

"Okay, okay. Don't get upset."

"How can I not be upset? I handpicked 'em. Taught
'em the business like they were my own . . ." Abe
trailed off. "It's not like it used to be. You can't trust
anybody anymore in this world. Not unless they're
blood."

"Slow down. You're jumping to conclusions here.
How do you *know* it's not a coincidence? It's not *that*
original an idea."

"My little voice over there was sworn to secrecy,
that's how. They got a lid on it. They don't want us
to know they know what we're doing. There's no
doubt about it. Somebody is feathering his nest."

"Does this kill the line for us?"

"Not if we move fast. But first we gotta get the *gonif*
out. That's your absolute top priority from this mo-

ment on, kiddo. Find out which one of 'em it is. Or
if it's both.''

"How?"

"By being a sneak, how else?"

"I'm not real good at that kind of—"

"We're all good at it when we're pushed. And we
been pushed. All right, pay attention: Lesson number . . . what number are we on?"

"I forget. Twenty-six."

"To stay ahead of your enemies you have to think
like your enemies."

"Doesn't that make you just like them?"

"No, it makes you smarter. Go to it."

"How?"

"You'll think of something. I have faith in you. Report when you have news."

"Okay Pop. I'll . . . I'll take care of it. You can count
on me.''

Danny hung up and slumped in the chair. It couldn't
be. Not one of the Turks. Not Irv. Not Larry. *Couldn't
be.* But *was.*

And to think he'd been ready to sell his half and go
in with them. Danny shuddered. Jesus, what had *that*
been? A hostile take-over bid? A squeeze play?

Danny jumped to his feet and began to pace around
the office. He was in over his head. How could Abe
trust him with a crisis like this on his first day? Think
like your enemies. Think like your enemies . . .

He rinsed his face in the little private washroom.
Looked at himself in the mirror. Big mistake. Someone who looked eighteen was not someone who was
capable of handling this. Why couldn't there be a back
door to Abe's office? He could slip right out, hop in
the car. Flee.

No, he couldn't. He was the boss.

Arrrghhh!!!

He combed his hair. He thought. And combed. And
thought. And when he had a plan, a good, sound

plan that he believed Abe would endorse, he steadied himself, buzzed Pip, and cooly informed her that Irv and Larry could come back in.

"So . . ." he began when they had taken their seats. "Where was I?"

"Something about an unforeseen development," suggested Larry, leaning forward eagerly.

"Oh, right. Believe it or not, my father has actually agreed to take my mother on a month-long trip to Israel for their twenty-fifth anniversary."

"No kidding? That's great!" said Irv. "He needs it."

"When are they leaving?" Larry wanted to know.

"Uh, today. They left this morning." Why couldn't he be a better liar?

"Sudden, wasn't it?" pressed Larry.

"Yeah. Kind of an impulsive thing. Anyway, he and I . . . we sort of patched things up before they left, at least to the extent that he asked me to look after things while he's gone. I have no idea what my role will be when he gets back. That's what I wanted to talk to you about. He and I . . . we still can't come to grips with our basic philosophical differences. We won't, not in this lifetime. My father isn't going to change. Not willingly. The only way he'll listen is if I sell my half. And that's what I've decided to do. You guys are right. It's the only way."

He waited for their reaction. Rather, he waited for Larry's reaction. Because it *was* Larry. Hyper, goony, polyester Larry. Two-faced, conniving, evil Larry. Scumbag Larry. Manipulating him. Manipulating Irv, too. Sure, that's what he did. He put Irv up to it, knowing that Danny liked and trusted Irv. No way it would look like something rotten if it came from Irv. And all the while . . .

Larry's reaction: he glanced over at Irv and smirked. He didn't even bother to hide it, the *schmuck*.

"The meeting's tomorrow morning."

Danny sat in a chair at the foot of Abe's bed, tie loosened, loafers off. It was a different room. Abe was
out of intensive care. Ev had gone home for the evening.

"Where?"

"Arnold's."

"Good work, kiddo. Fast work. Who's gonna be
there?"

"Me, the Turks, and the investors, whoever they turn
out to be."

"Lay you odds it'll be U-Buy. They want to con-
solidate us with Import Barn, make us into one big
chain. They're sharks. Shrewd idea you got, pretending you want to sell your half. Good way to smoke
the bastard out. I'd never have thought of it."

"Me either," Danny said quietly.

"What's that mean?"

Danny cleared his throat. "The Turks approached
me with the idea a while ago."

"Oh?" Abe arched an eyebrow. "How come you
didn't say something to me about it?"

Danny shrugged.

"You were considering it, weren't you, kiddo?" Abe
asked gravely.

"I-I guess I still have a lot to learn, Pop. I don't know
as much about people as I thought. As much as you
do. I'd have really screwed up the company if I'd had
the chance, if you hadn't happened to get sick. I may
still."

"No, you won't."

"I'm getting a real education here. My values matter a lot. But so do your insights, your experience.
I'm starting to respect those things a lot more."

"Know what a grownup is, kiddo? Somebody who
knows enough to know what he don't know, and to
admit it. This business has sure opened my eyes. The
fact that one of my Turks feels so cut off, so frus-
trated by me that he'd go behind my back . . ." Abe
shook his head. "You were right. I should have been

including them more in the decision-making process.
I blame myself for this. Any idea who it is?"

"Not for sure. I still need proof. You got good color
today, Pop."

"Ah, I'm bored."

"Watch some TV."

"Fooey."

"I thought about bringing you a nice greasy block
of cement and a scrub brush, but I ran out of time."

"Go ahead and laugh. When I'm dead you'll get more
for that house because it's been so well taken care
of."

"Stop talking like that, will ya? You're not going
anywhere."

Abe looked him over. "You lose some weight?"

"Maybe three pounds." Danny shifted in the chair.
"Why?"

"Nothing. It's good. Especially if heart disease runs
in the family. This have anything to do with Ruthie?"

"Rachel. It might."

"Good. Man in your position, you got better things
to worry about than finding a place to buy condoms
at eleven o'clock on a Saturday night."

Danny coughed. "Actually, I may be . . ."

"May be what?"

"I mean, *we* may be . . . sort of getting slightly
married."

"Whattya mean you *may* be. Are ya or aren't ya?"

"I are," Danny said.

"Atta boy. Now you're cooking with gas. Always
liked Rachel. Blond girl, right? Very clean-cut?"

"Mouse Stern's sister."

"Good. Got brains and looks both in that family.
Father's a doctor?"

"Dentist."

"Same thing. Point is she's not some loudmouthed
Shirley with dirty underwear who's after your dough."

"She's definitely not that."

"She got a job?"

"She's going to go to law school."

Abe nodded, impressed. "A professional girl. That's nice. So when are you—?"

"We don't know yet. Nothing's set, and we don't want to make any kind of big deal out of it, okay?"

"Sure, sure. We'll have to get you a house, though."

"We already have a—"

"Actually, why don't you just take the house? Mom and I can get a smaller—"

"There's time, okay?"

"Sure, sure."

"Pop, what do I say at this meeting tomorrow?"

"Nothing. You're there to look, to listen, and to act greedy. They don't know that you know. So keep your eyes and ears open. Concentrate. The littlest thing might give away who the *gonif* is."

"And if I find out? What then?"

"Up to you, kiddo. You're in charge now."

Danny and the Turks got to Arnold's Farmhouse a few minutes early. Irv got the three of them coffee. Danny kept his eyes on Larry, who sat across from him in his cocoa brown ensemble, nervously smoking a Kent.

Elliot Chadwick, the investment lawyer, was tanned and silver-haired and smooth. He wore a gray flannel suit with a hanky square in his pocket. He even smoked a pipe.

"A pleasure to meet you, Mr. Levine," he declared, gripping Danny's hand. "We've heard nothing but flattering things about you."

"From . . . ?"

"Your representatives, of course," he replied, his broad smile taking in both Larry and Irv. He sat. "What's good here?"

"Nothing," said Larry.

"Jell-O's not bad," Danny pointed out.

"I'll just have coffee." The lawyer looked around for a waiter.

"You have to serve yourself," advised Danny.

Irv started to get up. "Why don't I—?"

"No, no, I'll get it," Chadwick assured him. He strode briskly over to the steam tables, the heels of his wing tips rapping sharply on the linoleum.

Larry lit another Kent and flicked absently at the dandruff on his shoulders. Irv smiled tightly at Danny, who sipped at his coffee.

Chadwick returned, sat with his coffee, and set fire to his pipe. "So . . ."

"So make me an offer," said Danny, grinning.

Chadwick froze momentarily, then laughed. It was a laugh that came all the way up from the diaphragm. "Of course, you realize this is strictly an exploratory meeting. We're merely the legal representatives for the party that has expressed interest in investing in Pier West."

"Who's the 'we' you keep referring to?"

"My firm."

He produced a card and handed it across the table to Danny. It had the names of about eight partners in it. Offices were in the Union Oil Building downtown.

"We," continued Chadwick, "rather, I, am here to do the groundwork. Determine if there's mutual interest. Answer your questions. Then we proceed from there."

"Sounds good," said Danny.

Chadwick took a small flat leather notebook out of his inside jacket pocket, and a silver Cross pen. He opened the notepad and consulted it. "Yours is a wholly family-owned company?"

"Correct."

"We understand you hold title to fifty percent."

"Correct."

"Do you own it free and clear? By that I mean are there any attachments? Co-signers? If, ands, or buts?"

"Not since I turned twenty-one."

"And you're the sole heir?"

"Correct."

"No brothers or sisters?"

"Correct."

"You're a very lucky young fellow, aren't you?"

"Correct."

"I'm certain there are things you'd like to ask me."

Danny tugged at his ear. "Yes. For starters, who are you representing?"

Chadwick sat back, puffed on his pipe. "A party that has available investment capital. A party that would, provided there are no unforeseen impediments, be prepared to transfer to you the equivalent of six million dollars for your fifty percent of Pier West."

Six million dollars?!

"Hmmm . . ."

"Six-point-two-five is possible," Chadwick added quickly. "Anything higher than that we'd have to touch base with Minneapolis."

"What do you mean by an equivalent?"

"Stock. As well as stock options commensurate with your new position in the company. Over and above your salary, of course. Our party is a very solid, diversified, midwestern corporation, Mr. Levine. A Fortune 500 corporation, in fact. Providing investment capital is merely one of its many interests. It's also a major presence in the fields of agriculture, insurance, real estate development, consumer products—"

"Can you give me a for instance of some of the consumer products?"

"Certainly. There's Federated Foods, makers of—"

"I know what they make," grinned Danny, patting his belly. "Eat way too many of them."

"As well as Parker Pharmaceutical Laboratories, Wee Willie Toys, Arapahoe brand soft drinks, Mucho Taco restaurants, the U-Buy discount department stores—"

"U-Buy? They're pretty big now, huh?"

"Oh yes. They're in all fifty states, as well as Canada, Great Britain, and South Africa."

Danny drained his coffee. Chalk up one for Abe. Secretly U-Buy was already in the process of taking over Import Barn. Now it was after Pier West, too. And Larry was helping. Helping the big fish swallow the little ones. Positioning himself for a vault up into the Fortune 500. And to think Danny had almost helped him do it.

"I want to make sure my father's interests are protected," he said.

"Absolutely," Chadwick assured him. "We're not raiders, Mr. Levine. A seat on the board will have his name on it for as long as he wants it. You three gentlemen as well. Our party has no interest in forcing anyone out. Merely investing. Diversifying. It's a most uncertain world. Naturally, our party would expect to have its own members sitting on the board as well."

"But Pier West would retain its name?"

"I can't answer that for certain. I do know Pier West has excellent consumer identification value here on the West Coast, and that our party places a premium on that. In fact, it's not inconceivable that with our party's resources behind you, your consumer identification could grow into a national one."

"That would make my father very happy."

"I'm sure it would," agreed Chadwick wholeheartedly. "Anything else I can tell you?"

"As I said to Irv and Larry, I mainly wanted to meet you, Mr. Chadwick. Find out what your orientation is, get a clearer picture of what we're getting into here. I think I have that picture now. You're been a tremendous help in pointing me toward my decision. You'll be hearing from my legal representatives soon."

Chadwick put away his pen and notepad. "I'll look forward to it, sir."

"Thanks for coming all the way out here."

"No trouble. That's our job."

The four of them stood. Chadwick shook Danny's hand.

"Until later then, Mr. Levine. A pleasure to meet you."

"Likewise."

Mr. Chadwick also shook Irv's hand. "Mr. Green," he said. Lastly he shook Larry's hand. "And Mr. Borok. A pleasure meeting *you,* sir, too."

Danny's breath caught. Chadwick had never met Larry before. Irv was the one he knew. Irv was his contact.

Chadwick strode out of Arnold's. Then Irv turned to Danny and said, "Well, well. Very interesting, huh?"

Danny nodded. He couldn't speak.

Irv was the *gonif.*

The clock radio on Rachel's nightstand said it was 3:23. She was asleep. Rachel slept just like the dead—flat on her back, head straight, jaw slack, hands folded squarely across her stomach. She barely breathed. The first night he discovered this he got so frightened he woke her up.

He got up, stepped into a pair of shorts, and tip-toed into the kitchen. There he turned on the light and put the kettle on. Maybe a cup of hot water and milk would settle him down. He leaned against the counter and watched the blue flame under the kettle.

How could it be Irv? How could it be the guy he'd gotten stoned with, talked politics with, shared dreams with? How could it be the father of Abraham? How could it be Irv?

Danny watched the flame and wondered.

"Change your mind?"

He hadn't heard her come in. She stood there in her old oversized Dewey Weber T-shirt, golden hair tou-sled, blinking from the light. God, she was cute. Was it possible he would ever stop thinking that? No, it was not.

He forced a smile. "Change my mind about what?"
"Us."

"Uh-uh." He slumped down into one of the dining chairs, put his elbows on the table, and rested his chin on his fists.

She sat across from him, put her elbows on the table, and rested her chin on her fists. "What is it?"

"Nothing."

"Then what are you—?"

"Business. No big deal."

"Oh," she said coldly.

"Okay," he admitted. "I'm being a fucking Jewish male again."

She didn't contradict him.

Danny sat back, sighed. She liked Irv. The news would upset her. He couldn't bear to upset her. "It's a personnel thing. I may have to fire someone for tipping off the competition."

"Who?"

"Import Barn."

"No, I meant—"

"You don't know the person. The thing is, I never fired anybody before."

"First time for everything, I guess."

"I guess."

She came over to him, rubbed his neck. He bowed his head.

"When do you want to do it?" she asked.

"First thing in the morning. Get it over with as soon as possible."

"I meant the wedding."

"First thing in the morning. Get it over with as soon as possible."

She laughed. He pulled her down onto his lap and held her. It was nice sitting there like that, just the two of them together in their own house. Long ago he had dreamt of moments like this. And now it was real. If only he didn't have so damned much on his mind.

He kissed her. "Soon as you want."

"Can we not have people? I hate weddings."

"So do I. No reason to think I'd like this one any better just because it's my own. We'll just invite the parents, Mouse and Wendy . . ."

"And a judge," she added. "No rabbi."

"Uh . . ."

"I don't want a rabbi."

"I don't either."

"Then it's settled," she concluded, pleased.

"I do have to point out that my pop will be really upset if we don't have one," Danny said.

"Is that why we're getting married? To make your father happy?"

"No . . ."

"If we have a rabbi it'll be a Jewish wedding. And we will be performing seals."

"We're not performing seals," Danny countered. "Besides, that's only if you have three hundred people and musicians and cocktail weenies. We won't. We don't need gifts. We don't need any of that. We don't even need to get married, if you get right down to it."

"So why are we?" she demanded.

"I guess I'm a tiny bit old-fashioned," he confessed.

"That the only reason?"

"I'm also kind of totally nuts about you."

Rachel softened. "I love you so much, Danny."

"Rooms, did you . . . did you ever say that to Rick?"

"Yes," she replied quietly. "But I never meant it."

"Now you do?"

"Yes."

"How do you know?"

"I know."

"What if you change your mind?"

"Why should I?"

"Well, for starters, I'm not really the world's brightest person. I don't get people."

"No one does, silly."

"They don't?"

"Uh-uh. At least you *want* to." She frowned. "You okay?"

He nodded. "Just feeling a little . . ."

"Insecure?"

"Fat."

"Tell you what—the cookies are in the linen closet. You may have *one*."

He grinned. "Gee, I'm going to get spoiled. Look, this rabbi thing, it doesn't mean much to me. But it does mean a lot to the folks. I think we have to respect that. Pop's health isn't great, and he's earned the right to—"

"It's *our* wedding."

"I know."

"We're having a judge, or we're not having it at all."

Danny sighed inwardly. She was not, he sensed, going to budge on this. "Okay. We're having a judge. I'll break it to him."

"You'll be firm?"

"Hey, I'm the boss." He kissed her on the nose. "This means I get two cookies though."

"Deal." She pushed up out of his lap. "I'm going back to bed."

Danny held her there by the hand. He had to tell her about Irv. There shouldn't be secrets between them. "Rooms?"

"Yes?" She smiled. There was a glow to her. She was healing, happy.

He released her hand, puffed out his cheeks. "G'night."

"Morning, boss," Pip said brightly as she came in, arms full, and began dumping things on the desk in front of him. "Sales figures for last week. Assorted inner-office memoranda. The Czar's personal correspondence. Coffee."

"No doughnut?"

She frowned. "Now you want one?"

"No, I want two. And I'd like Irv Green to come see me in ten minutes. That should give me just enough time to eat both doughnuts and then to vomit."

"Whatever you say," she said, mystified.

She returned a minute later with his doughnuts and proceeded to tidy up the desk, lingering in case Danny wanted to explain himself. When she gathered he didn't, she scurried out.

Irv's timing was perfect. Danny was just finished gargling in the washroom when he came in. Danny motioned for him to sit.

"So what did you think of Chadwick?" Irv asked.

"Seemed okay," called Danny.

"A slick operator, I thought. But I suppose those are the kind of people we have to get used to dealing with."

"I suppose."

"Pip said you wanted to—"

"Talk." Danny closed the office door. "I need you to help me with an ethical matter."

Irv grinned. "Right up my alley."

Danny sat behind the big desk, cleared his throat, found a train penny and rubbed it. "There's something I'm trying to understand, but just don't," he began slowly. "How is it that a guy who wears a workshirt and has a beard and smokes dope and is into the Dead . . . a guy who feels the same way I do about the war, business, a guy who's a *friend* . . . How is it possible that he isn't cool? That he's nothing like he appears to be. That he really only cares about himself. How is that possible?"

Irv's forehead creased. "Can you be more specific?"

"I can be very specific."

They stared at each other.

"Oh," Irv said quietly.

Danny nodded. "Oh."

"You're not really selling your—?"

"No, I'm not."

Irv nodded. "How did you find out? Somebody over at the Barn?"

"That doesn't matter. What matters is how you could do it, Irv. How could you betray the company, my dad, me? Explain it to me. I don't get it."

"That doesn't surprise me. Things are a lot different for you. A number of us weren't born with a front office position waiting for us."

"I know that. I wasn't born that way either. There was no Pier West when I was a kid. My pop built it. Worked hard. Worked honestly. He may be old-fashioned now. Possibly a little insensitive. Certainly more than a little maddening. But one thing he's not is a crud. He's decent. You'd have sold what he built right out from under him. Him and me."

"It's not personal."

"It's very personal. It damn well is." Danny shook his head. "I thought you were like me. I thought you believed the things I believe."

"I do believe them, Danny. I wasn't jerking your chain."

"Then how can you justify what you've done?"

"I don't have to," Irv replied. "This is business, man. The only operating ethic of business is that there is no ethic. It's strictly survival of the fittest. The sharpest and toughest make it. The rest don't. That's what's so beautiful about it. It's the last great American frontier. No rules. No restraints, at least none that are enforced. You're free to go as far as your nerve and skill and luck will take you. Business *works.* It's the only institution in this country that still does."

"But you wanted to do good things. Make the company socially responsible. Take an active role in public policy."

"I still do. Someday I will."

"How *can* you if you conduct yourself like this?!"

"It's the only way I can get my shot. That's how it works."

"Not necessarily," Danny argued. "Here, you would have gotten your shot. Gotten it fair and square. And *how* you get it *matters*. Method isn't something you can just toss in the trash when it becomes a bother. We're talking about a set of beliefs here, not an ant farm. We're talking about what's supposed to make us different."

Irv raised an eyebrow. *"Us?"*

Danny flushed. "Look, Irv, this has never been an issue between us, but . . . I can't pretend to know what it's like to be black. I realize you have a whole set of hurdles and pressures that I can't possibly comprehend. I'm trying to understand you. I really am. But from where I'm sitting what you've done only makes sense to me one way."

"Which is . . . ?"

"You're a total asshole."

Irv let out a short laugh. "No, I'm not. I'm a good husband. Good father. Good citizen. I'm just realistic, that's all."

"I'm very disappointed in you. I'm hurt. And I'm pissed off. You've spoiled the Grateful Dead for me, and that's a terrible thing to do to anyone. Should have listened to my pop. That was my big mistake."

"He suspected something?"

"Not a thing. But he would have, if he'd made the effort to get to know you better. See, he taught me two things when I was little that really stuck. One was that it's always hottest in L.A. right around the Jewish holidays. Two was never, ever trust a man who doesn't like baseball. I trusted you. That's a mistake I'll never make again."

They stared at each other some more.

"So . . . ?" Irv finally said.

"So you'd better go home and tell Charlene and little Abraham that you don't work here anymore," Danny said. "I expect Import Barn will take you in. I expect that was your plan all along. Dunno. Good-bye."

Irv stood up. "I know you won't believe this, Danny, but I'm going to miss working with you. I respect you. I respect your principles."

"I'm going to miss working with you, too, Irv. Try to be out of your office by noon. After that the lock will be changed. Send Larry in when you pass his office, would you?"

"For what it's worth, Larry merely followed my—"

"You know, in a weird sort of way I'm glad this happened. You've convinced me I'm making the right move by staying on here, being a businessman. Because if I don't, if I step aside, just hang out, then this country will end up being run entirely by people like you."

"It still will. It's the way."

"Then it's time for a change."

"You honestly think you can make a difference?"

"Always have."

"Good luck, Danny. You're in for an extremely rude awakening."

Irv left. Danny watched him as he went down the hall, stopping in Larry's office. A moment later Larry came flying out. He was ashen by the time he made it to Abe's office. His hands shook. "W-what's . . . ?" he stammered. "I-Irv just said that he's . . . that you . . ."

"Sit, Larry," Danny commanded.

Larry sat.

"I don't believe you're dishonest or devious," Danny told him. "You just let Irv talk you into something. I'm prepared to consider it an error in judgment and to not hold it against you. But if you ever give me the *slightest* reason to think I'm wrong, you're *fired*! Understand?"

Heads were sticking out doorways all the way down the hall. He hadn't asked Larry to shut the door. Too late now.

"Yessir, M-Mr. Levine," Larry said.

"Now get out. Please."

"Right away." Larry jumped to his feet and lurched out awkwardly.

Pip came in a moment later and stood across the desk from him, her eyes narrowed. "I don't believe it," she said. "Czar II lives."

"Don't ever say that to me again," snapped Danny.

She reddened. "Just trying to lighten things up. I know you're . . ." She eyed the carpet at her feet.

"Take a memo, please. On American Heritage."

She sat, pad and pen ready.

"To all staff," Danny began. " 'It's time for us to get rolling on this new line. A company-wide commitment will be required if we're to be in the stores for the bicentennial. Please be prepared to make this your top priority. Thank you for your cooperation. Danny.' That'll be all, Pip."

"Don't you want to set up a meeting?"

"What for? There's no one here who's either smart enough or trustworthy enough to be of any help at this stage. I'll handle it myself."

"Whatever you say, Mr. Levine," she said icily.

Danny relaxed. Good old Pip. Smart, loyal, tough Pip. "With your input, of course. Without you, I'm lost."

"Just so you know it," she said. "For a second I thought you forgot. Just like you forgot that the way to get full cooperation from people is to include them in the creative end. That way they'll feel like it's *their* project."

"You're right. You're absolutely right. Lost my head for a second. Whew, that was a close one, huh?"

"Very. Ten o'clock be okay?"

"Ten o'clock will be just fine."

"Anything else, boss?"

"Yes, Pip. Don't ever leave."

Chapter Fifteen

A very small engagement party was held at the house the Saturday Abe came home from the hospital. Just a couple of glasses of champagne out on the patio. No frills, the way Danny and Rachel wanted it. Mouse and Wendy were there. Dr. and Mrs. Stern. Some assorted cold cuts. And lots of approval.

Mrs. Stern kissed Danny on the mouth. Dr. Stern took his jaw in his hand and commanded "Bite" so he could see if Danny's teeth had stayed straight. They had. "Still my best patient," beamed his future father-in-law.

Danny and Rachel stood next to the pool holding hands. She seemed very cheerful. Danny made the first toast.

"I'd like to drink to my pop," he said, holding his glass up, "who gave all of us a scare."

Abe grunted. This was Abe's new thing, grunting. He also had a new mannerism for whenever Danny told him something he didn't want to hear—he'd touch his chest and wince slightly. That was just what he'd done when Danny told him they wanted to be married by a judge instead of a rabbi. Touched his chest.

Winced. And replied, with weary resignation, "Whatever you want, kiddo. I'll tell Mom." So Danny put
his foot down—it was a rabbi or nothing, he told
Rachel. She said fine and the wedding was called off.
A day later they compromised. Rabbi Waldman
would perform the ceremony. He was really almost
family, if you got right down to it. And it would be
a civil, non-religious ceremony—no *chupa,* no glass to
step on, no guests.

Dr. Stern toasted the happy couple.

"It pleases me very, very much," he said, "to see
two old friends join together like this. This is not an
impulse. It's a kinship, an understanding, a *bond* that,
like a fine wine, will grow deeper and mellower
through the years."

"Hear, hear!" everyone called out.

It was a nice toast, and Danny swore it sounded familiar. There was a good reason for that—Dr. Stern
made the same toast at Mouse and Wendy's wedding
reception.

Abe's turn came next.

"Kiddo," he said, "you've made Mom and me very
proud. You've taken your rightful place. And now,
most important of all, you've found a nice girl. A girl
who's maybe even too good for ya. I been thinking
about the future a lot lately. I've had time to think . . ."

"C'mon, Pop. Chin up!" Danny called out.

Abe waved him off. "No, no, I been thinking. And
when I look at the two of ya standing here today,
I—I *see* the future. And . . ." Abe trailed off. A funny
noise came out of him. Danny realized he was actually choking back tears. At once Danny found himself
doing the same. "And I'm . . . I'm *not worried.*" Abe
blinked several times. "Anyway, *mazel tov* to the both
of you," he concluded hurriedly, blowing his nose
in a cocktail napkin.

Then it came time for some real surprises.

Mouse and Wendy asked for silence.

"Speaking of taking your rightful place, Mr. Levine . . ." Wendy began proudly.

"You can call him Abe now," Danny assured her. "You're family."

Abe grunted.

"I would like to congratulate my very gifted husband who has been promoted to a full-fledged partnership in the Allied Talent Agency, complete with his very own American Express card and client list."

"Hear, hear!" everyone yelled.

Mouse took Wendy's hand. "Please. Let's forget the office, talk about something that matters."

"You feeling okay, Stern?" joshed Danny.

Mouse cackled. "Do you mind, Levine? A person is trying to make an announcement here." Mouse held up his glass. "I'd like you to join me in raising your glasses to my sweet, darling wife, who informed me this morning that she's about to present me with the gift of life."

Ev and Mrs. Stern shrieked with delight. Rachel just shrieked and dug her nails into Danny's hand.

Danny stood beside the pool, stunned and amazed. Stunned by the idea of Mouse Stern as someone's father. Amazed that he, Danny Levine, was standing right next to nine feet of cool blue water during a relatively important occasion and he wasn't afraid of falling in. He wasn't going to fall in. He was a grownup now. He was also holding onto Rachel, and Rachel wasn't ever going to fall in.

She went to congratulate Wendy. He went over to Abe and put his arm around him. "I was very touched by what you said, Pop. Made me feel loved."

"Let's not get all huggy and kissy," sniffed Abe. "Can't stand families that are into that crap."

Danny grinned. "Whatever you say, Pop."

Abe glanced over at the guests, led Danny a few feet away from them. "Listen, kiddo," he said confidentially, "I don't want you to take this as a criticism of the job you're doing but our friend Irv Green is suing us."

Danny gulped, horrified. *"What?!"*

"Ssh. You'll upset the women. Our lawyers called me this morning—"

"I thought they were going to call *me* from now on."

"Force of habit. Apparently, he's saying we *yentzed* him without just cause, and thereby violated his civil rights, which are now protected by one of those new goddamned equal opportunity laws."

"But it's not true!"

"I know that. I told them what happened."

"He has no case, right?"

"I'm sorry to say he does."

Danny examined his shoes. "No, I'm the one who's sorry. I guess maybe you'd better bring in someone who knows what he's doing. I thought I—"

"No, no, don't take it that way, kiddo. Not anything you did wrong, believe me. You handled the situation very well. But it's strictly hands off with black employees now unless you got a tight case, and we don't. It's our word against his. Nothing on paper, except his personnel record, which is flawless. And Import Barn sure as hell won't bail us out by testifying on our behalf."

"I figured he'd go over there."

"According to my little voice they don't trust him either."

"So what do the lawyers advise?"

"If we let him take us to court it'll cost us a fortune, even if we win. And we won't win."

"So we settle?"

"So we take him back."

"No. Absolutely not."

"We have no choice, kiddo. It's the luck of the draw. If it'd been Larry we'd be home free. Irv we're stuck with. That's the law. Can't stash him in the mailroom, either. He has to be restored to an equivalent job at his previous salary and be compensated for the time he missed."

Danny shook his head. "This is crazy."

"Crazy," agreed Abe. "Lesson number . . . what number are we on?"

"Thirty-two."

"Even when you're in charge you're not in charge—there's always a higher authority. These days, it happens to be your red tape."

"It's not *my* red tape," grumbled Danny.

Abe patted him on the back. "It is now, D.L. . . . Just don't let it get to you."

Danny nodded and stormed the buffet table. A triple-decker calmed him, at least enough so he could go over and shake Mouse's hand. "Great news, Stern," he exclaimed. "A father. Wow."

"Thanks, Levine. Hey, whattya think, we old enough now to call each other by our first names? Can the gym class shit? Huh, *Danny?*"

"Sure . . . *Mike.*"

"What the hell—it'll keep Wendy happy. She needs a role in life. That's what's been bugging her. Now she'll have one. She'll be the mother of my child. Only one thing bothers me—what if it's a boy and he gets my looks?"

"You haven't done so bad . . . Mike."

"Guess I haven't at that." Mouse glanced over at Wendy, who was engaged in bubbly conversation with the two mothers and Rachel. "Mandy's out of the picture now, I tell ya?"

"No kidding?"

"Yeah, I dumped her," Mouse said, very offhanded. "Typical Hollywood slut. Don't know how I—"

"She dumped you, huh?"

"Some cameraman name of Sven," Mouse admitted sourly. "Six feet five. Fuck it, I ain't got the clout to hold onto 'em. Not yet."

"Dunno, Mike, there's a pretty decent lady over there

you can hold onto for a real long time, if you're nice enough to her."

"What, *you're* giving *me* advice now?"

"Can I ask you something personal, Mike?"

"Sure."

"Did you ever actually sleep with Mandy?"

Mouse reddened, started to answer, stopped. Started to answer, stopped. Then he cackled. "Sure did think about it a lot."

"I'll bet. Separate rooms in Vegas?"

Mouse nodded. "Must have jerked off nine times in two days. It won't be long now, though. I'm on my way. You watch. Pretty soon I'll be banging every single one of 'em. Banging 'em good."

"Sure you will, Mike. So this promotion is a good thing, huh? You'll have famous clients and stuff?"

"Not right away. I'm out of the talent end—they got me handling writers now. And a couple of directors. One's actually younger than we are. Just did a *Night Gallery* segment with Joan Crawford, who I thought was dead. What the hell, at least we'll be able to afford a house on the right side of the hill now. Place like this. This is nice."

"My pop wants to give it to us as a wedding present."

"Boychick, I have just two words of advice—take it."

Next, Danny cornered Wendy and gave her a hug. "What a gal!" he exclaimed.

"Thanks, Wuggy."

"I'm so happy you're working things out. It's really right. And a *kid*."

"It wasn't easy, let me tell you. First I had to get him drunk. Then I had to call him dirty—"

"That's a private moment. Don't share it, really. The point is, now the two of you will have something to build toward. A family."

"What if we're doing the wrong thing? I don't even know for sure that he loves me."

"In his own way, he does. You just have to wait him out. You'll see. He may even turn out to be the greatest father in the world. Weirder things have happened." He watched Rachel, who was talking to Ev. "If you wait long enough, people do come around."

Afterward, when the two of them were driving down the canyon toward home, he asked Rachel what she was thinking.

"I'm thinking," she said, "how much I don't want to have kids."

"Funny, I was thinking the same thing."

"Let's not, Danny. Ever."

"Agreed."

"Promise?"

"Absolutely. All they do is cry at night and shit on you and tie you down. That's not what I want out of life. That's strictly for other people. Parents."

"Then it's a deal?" she asked.

"Deal."

They shook hands on it.

"Gee," remarked Danny, pleased. "That one was easy."

It felt good to be back up in Newt's treehouse. The smell of the avocado tree. The cool dampness. The view through the leaves of the old bomb shelter, where he'd slept when he lived there. He sure did spend a lot of nights up here with Newt, talking about life and women and stuff. It was in this very treehouse that Danny had set one-half of his hair on fire trying to light that kazoo hash pipe. He certainly had looked odd for the next several weeks. Ah, memories.

It was early evening. An empty beer can with cigarette butts in it sat at his feet, along with a paperback copy of *Journey to the Center of the Earth* by Jules Verne. One of Newt's favorites.

Danny picked up the book and opened it to the marked place. Newt had underlined in red the long-lost message that Professor Lindenbrock and his courageous nephew, Axel, unearthed from an ancient parchment:

> *Descend into the crater of Sneffels Yokul over which*
> *the shadow of Scartaris falls before the calends of July,*
> *bold traveller, and you will reach the center of the*
> *earth. I have done this.*
> *Arne Saknussemm*

A warm feeling passed over Danny. Those *were* some pretty good, strange times he and Newt had shared. More than that. Friendship. The kind that stayed alive no matter where they were or what they were doing. He hadn't been wrong to leave Newt. He'd needed to follow his own path, and he had. Newt probably knew where it would lead him all along. Newt seemed to understand such things.

Danny heard footsteps in the leaves below. It was almost dark now, but he could make out Newt's long, loping gait.

"Peenis," he called down.

Newt stopped. "Daniel?" he called up, surprised.

"You gave our password to somebody else?" Danny demanded, indignant.

"No, no," Newt assured him. "I merely . . . permission to come aboard, sir."

"Not until you say the password."

"Peeenis."

"Permission granted."

Newt came up by the rope, arm over arm. Danny made room as he squeezed in next to him on the sturdy wooden seat.

"What brings you by, Daniel?"

"Nothing much. Getting married."

"Congratulations."

"Thanks. I'd invite you to the wedding, if you'd come."

"Thanks anyway." Newt began to tap his foot nervously. He took out a cigarette and lit it with a kitchen match. The flame illuminated his Biddle face, and when Danny saw it he grabbed the match from Newt.

Newt had been beaten up. One eye was blackened and swollen half-shut. His lower lip was fat and scabbed. So was one ear.

"Jesus, what happened?" Danny cried.

Newt looked away. "Nothing much."

"Bullshit." The match burned at Danny's fingers. He shook it out. "Tell me."

"A petty scrape with some lowlife dealers. No big deal."

"I want you to give serious thought to pulling out of this."

"I'm fine," Newt assured him.

"You're not fine. You still tripping?"

"Daniel, please don't judge what you can't understand."

"I understand totally. You're running away."

"I'm running *to* something."

"And what's that?"

"The absolute truth."

Danny shook his head. "No, you're not."

"I know what I'm doing," Newt insisted, Biddle chin stuck stubbornly out.

"Listen, Newt . . . How can I put this? You want a job?"

"Don't be ridiculous."

"I'm not. There's nobody there who's smart, who I can trust. I need you. I really do. We could have a lot of fun. Do a lot of the things you've talked about doing—only *real*."

"Thank you, but no."

"I hate to see you like this, Newt. I care about you."

"Don't," Newt said coldly.

They sat there in silence. Often they'd sat together

for long stretches in comfortable silence. This wasn't
so comfortable.

"Okay," Danny said finally. "I guess I'll be going."

"As you wish."

Danny chose the secure ladder over the rope. He
started down, searching carefully with his foot for
the rung.

"Daniel?"

Danny stopped. "Yeah, Newt?"

"Who is it you're marrying?"

"Rachel Stern. Mouse's sister."

"Of course. The one with the mustache."

"She does *not* have a mustache. That's not hair, it's
down. Fine, blond down."

"Of course it is. My mistake."

"See ya, Newt."

"Until the revolution, Daniel."

Danny's fear yanked him awake in the middle of
the night. A major pang of it. Cold sweats. Pounding
heart. *Fear.*

He clenched and unclenched his fists. He took several deep breaths in and out. And when none of that
did any good he poked Rachel.

She stirred. "Hmm?" she murmured heavily.
"Wha . . . ?"

"Are we any different?"

"Different than what?" she wondered, yawning.

"Mouse and Wendy."

"Yes." She seemed awake now. "We're happy."

"We are?"

"I am."

"So am I. That's right. We *are* different. We're
happy. Gee, thanks, Rooms." Danny felt himself relax. She'd made his fear go away, just like when Ev
chased away the bogeyman who hid behind his bedroom closet door when he was little. "Sorry I woke
you. Go back to sleep. Oh, wait, there's something

I have to tell you. Know that personnel thing? That person I had to fire? That was Irv."

"I know it was," she said.

"How? Did my—?"

"I know you. Who else would you have been so upset over firing?"

"As it turns out, I didn't fire him. I can't. He's taking advantage of a law that's there to fight racial discrimination. It was a real battle to get that law enacted, and he's abusing it, and that's wrong, and I'm getting screwed. It's very confusing. The more I think about it the more confused I get. My pop says you can't get upset over things you can't control. You have to concentrate on the things you *can* control. That was lesson number—"

"That's an excuse for apathy."

"Or sanity."

"You've got to get upset," Rachel insisted.

"I do?"

"If you don't you'll be just like everyone else. We'll be just like everyone else."

"Maybe we are," said Danny. "Maybe we're just fooling ourselves, thinking we're so different. Maybe everybody fools themselves that way. So they can get on with their lives. So they can get to sleep at night. Is that possible?"

"No," she replied gravely. "It isn't possible."

"It isn't," he agreed, taking her hand. "I owe you an apology. I'm sorry I didn't tell you before about Irv. I didn't want you to . . . I mean, I was afraid you'd—"

"I'm not made out of crystal. I won't break."

"I know."

"You'll tell me next time?"

"I'll . . ."

"You'll what?"

"I'll sure try."

She snuggled against him, kissed him lazily on the mouth. "G'night, Rooms."

"G'night, Rooms," he said, kissing her back. Then he turned over, buried his head in his pillow, and was instantly asleep.

They were on Sunset in the MG, nearing the strip. Danny wasn't sure where they were heading exactly. Mouse was being very mysterious.

"I hope you didn't go to any trouble," Danny said. "You really didn't have to."

"Nonsense. You had me a party. Now it's my turn." He cackled, clearly tickled to death. "Here. Turn in here."

It was a hotel, the Continental Hyatt House. Someone at the door took the MG. An elevator whisked them up to the eighth floor.

"What *is* all this, Mike?" Danny pressed.

"You'll see, boychick. And you'll do a helluva lot more, too."

The key in Mouse's pocket opened the door to room 806. It was dark inside. Mouse flicked on the lights to reveal five young women of assorted races lounging about on sofas, drinking champagne. They were naked, except for cowboy hats and high-heeled boots.

"Evening, ladies," Mouse called out. "Now the party may begin."

They squealed with delight, ran to greet Danny and Mouse with hugs and kisses and eager fingers.

"Like the hats?" Mouse asked him.

Danny extricated himself, swallowed. "Hats? What hats?"

"Cost a few extra bucks, but what the hell, huh?"

"Stern?"

"No last names anymore, remember?"

"Mike?"

"Yes, Danny?"

"You're all class."

"I am that. Now for the ground rules." Mouse whipped off his cardigan and hurled it to the carpet. "This black bitch is mine. Otherwise, it's every man for himself."

"There's just us two?" Danny asked.

"Would you really want to share this with someone else?"

Danny heard a rustling sound coming from the bedroom. He went to investigate, returned. "Mike, there's a midget in the bedroom reading the *Herald Examiner*."

"That's for later," Mouse replied as he settled down onto the sofa amid the black woman. "Entertainment."

A blonde brought Danny a glass of champagne. He accepted it, stood there sipping it.

"C'mon, Danny boy," urged Mouse. "Take your pick."

"Um . . . I hope you won't take this the wrong way, but could we just sort of go somewhere and talk?"

Mouse frowned. "Talk? Why would you want to talk when you could do this instead?"

"It's what I'm in the mood to do."

"You serious?"

"Yes."

With tremendous reluctance Mouse said "Okay. It's your party. If that's what you *really* want . . ."

"That's what I really want."

"We'll go for a drive."

"Thanks. I knew you'd understand."

"Who understands?"

They drove up Laurel Canyon to Lookout Mountain, the same spot they went to the night before Mouse got married. They brought the champagne with them. Danny parked and they drank it, looking down at the lights of the city.

"Better?" Mouse asked.

"Uh-huh."

"What's on your mind?"

"I just never thought this would happen to me, that's all."

"You never thought what would happen to you?"

"*This*. This life. It used to be what I was most afraid of."

"What is it now?"

"It's what's right in front of me," said Danny.

"There you are then," said Mouse. "It's not so bad. Take the step. You'll see. Just take the step."

It was bright and very hot the day Danny and Rachel got married. The Jewish holidays were, after all, just around the corner. Rabbi Waldman performed the ceremony under a *chupa* set up in Dr. and Mrs. Stern's yard. Danny and Rachel both freaked out when they saw the *chupa* there. The parents had double-crossed them. Parents could be very sneaky that way—they knew the happy couple would have no choice but to go through with it. There were plane and hotel reservations to think of. Danny's desk was even cleaned off.

The ceremony was over very fast. It was just past noon when the big fella took the step and the glass, which was wrapped inside a cloth napkin, shattered under his foot.

A large piece of the glass tore right through the napkin.

It tore right through the sole of Danny's loafer, too.

Eleven stitches closed the wound. Danny was on crutches in Maui, his injured foot in a clean sweat sock. He had to stay off the beach for fear of getting an infection. Otherwise it was a very nice honeymoon. Rachel looked lovely in her new bikini. And Danny felt a new calm. It wasn't the painkillers he was taking four times a day to keep his foot from pulsing, pulsing, pulsing. It was his Fear—it was gone. Mouse had been right. All he had to do was take the step. There was nothing to be afraid of.

Danny's Fear was behind him now. He didn't have to worry about it anymore. All he had to worry about now was that he would blow it: he would not get American Heritage into the stores before Import Barn did. Pier West would go under. Five hundred and fifty people would be thrown out of work. It would all be his fault.

But this didn't frighten Danny. Danny could deal with this. This was *tsuris*. His *tsuris*.

TITLES OF THE AVAILABLE PRESS
in order of publication

THE CENTAUR IN THE GARDEN, a novel by Moacyr Scliar
EL ANGEL'S LAST CONQUEST, a novel by Elvira Orphée
A STRANGE VIRUS OF UNKNOWN ORIGIN, a study by
    Dr. Jacques Leibowitch
THE TALES OF PATRICK MERLA, short stories by Patrick Merla
ELSEWHERE, a novel by Jonathan Strong
THE AVAILABLE PRESS/PEN SHORT STORY COLLECTION
CAUGHT, a novel by Jane Schwartz
THE ONE-MAN ARMY, a novel by Moacyr Scliar
THE CARNIVAL OF THE ANIMALS, short stories by Moacyr Scliar
LAST WORDS AND OTHER POEMS, poetry by Antler
O'CLOCK, short stories by Quim Monzó
MURDER BY REMOTE CONTROL, a novel in pictures
    by Janwillem van de Wetering and Paul Kirchner
VIC HOLYFIELD AND THE CLASS OF 1957, a novel by William Heyen
AIR, a novel by Michael Upchurch
THE GODS OF RAQUEL, a novel by Moacyr Scliar
SUTERISMS, pictures by David Suter
DOCTOR WOOREDDY'S PRESCRIPTION FOR ENDURING
    THE END OF THE WORLD, a novel by Colin Johnson
THE CHESTNUT RAIN, a poem by William Heyen
THE MAN IN THE MONKEY SUIT, a novel by Oswaldo França, Júnior
KIDDO, a novel by David Handler
COD STREUTH, a novel by Bamber Gascoigne
LUNACY & CAPRICE, a novel by Henry Van Dyke
HE DIED WITH HIS EYES OPEN, a mystery by Derek Raymond
DUSTSHIP GLORY, a novel by Andreas Schroeder
FOR LOVE, ONLY FOR LOVE, a novel by Pasquale Festa Campanile
'BUCKINGHAM PALACE,' DISTRICT SIX, a novel by Richard Rive
THE SONG OF THE FOREST, a novel by Colin Mackay
BE-BOP, RE-BOP, a novel by Xam Wilson Cartier
THE BALAD OF THE FALSE MESSIAH, a novel by Moacyr Scliar
little pictures, short stories by andrew ramer
THE DEVIL'S HOME ON LEAVE, a mystery by Derek Raymond